MW01600356

UNTIL I COME BACK FOR YOU

EARLY PRAISE FOR
UNTIL I COME BACK FOR YOU

"It was engrossing, charming, and so funny and surprising and I could just feel your energy from the start. Also, now I suspect that it's all true. Lol."
—BESTIE

"Loved it! This is just a great piece of authentic literature."
—HIGH SCHOOL FRIEND

"If it weren't for the murder, this would be a really cute story."
—NEIGHBOR

"HOLY SHIT...You wrote a book! Congratulations! I'm sitting here with tears running down my face because I loved this story so damn much!"
—EDITOR

"This story is amazing. Riveting! Fascinating! I think it will be on the NYT best seller list! Well, that list is BS, but you get my point."
—GRAD SCHOOL FRIEND

"If even ten percent of this is true, I want to hug you."
—FRIEND

"Loved loved loved it. The character development and imagery made it so enjoyable, I felt like I was right there through the whole book."
—COLLEGE ROOMMATE

"It's definitely in my pile."
—FORMER COWORKER

"I giggled, laughed, felt anxious, worried, relieved, sad, happy—you name it. I felt it all."
—CHILDHOOD FRIEND

"This would make a damned fine movie, and I'm not just saying that. It's edge-of-your-seat good."
—FRIEND

"This story made me laugh, cry, and cringe."
—BOOK CLUB LADY

"Didn't have time to read."
—BROTHER

"You don't read much, do you?"
—SISTER

"I had no idea you were this bad as a kid."
—OTHER SISTER

"You wrote a book?"
—MOM

"We appreciate the opportunity to review your work. Unfortunately, we didn't connect quite strongly enough with the pages to be your best next foot forward."
—GILLIAN FLYNN'S AGENCY

UNTIL I COME BACK FOR YOU

DEBUT NOVEL BY

P.A. WHITE

LUMINARE PRESS
WWW.LUMINAREPRESS.COM

This book is a work of autofiction, combining elements of auto-biography and fiction. While inspired by experiences from the author's childhood, it is a work of fiction. Significant elements of the story, including names, characters, incidents, and dialogue, have been fictionalized and embellished for dramatic effect. All names, except those of the author's immediate family, have been changed to protect the privacy and identities of the individuals portrayed. Any resemblance to actual persons, living or dead, or events is purely coincidental.

UNTIL I COME BACK FOR YOU
Copyright © 2025 by P.A. White

All rights reserved. This book or any portion thereof may not be reproduced or used in any manner whatsoever without the express written permission of the author, except for the use of brief quotations in a book review.

Cover photo by Spencer Selover (IG selover_visuals)

Printed in the United States of America

Luminare Press
442 Charnelton St.
Eugene, OR 97401
www.luminarepress.com

LCCN: 2024925105
ISBN: 979-8-88679-747-3

---

https://www.facebook.com/PAWhiteWrites

All proceeds from the sale of this book will be donated to horse rescues and other animal charities.

*For my siblings, who believed—
nay, expected—I would do great things. They are
the reason I didn't have monsters under my bed
until I was strong enough to defeat them.*

Pause you who read this, and think for a moment
of the long chain of iron or gold, of thorns or flowers,
that would never have bound you, but for the formation
of the first link on one memorable day.

—CHARLES DICKENS, *Great Expectations*

Prologue

———•———

Ronnie Clark didn't have to die that day.

Not really.

Ronnie Clark was a mean son of a bitch, and he deserved to be punished for the cruel, hateful shit he did. And if there is a hell, I suspect he's still there.

But he didn't have to die.

Not really.

If only he hadn't cussed in front of my mom.

No, she didn't kill him. That blood will always be on my hands. But when he cussed to my mom's face, he set his own feet on that path.

Proverbs says a man's heart plans his course. And man, you just don't cuss in front of my mom.

It wasn't even just that he cussed—it was how he did. I mean, he could have gotten away with *damn*, *dammit*, *ass*, and maybe even *shit*. But he went too far.

He used the f-word.

In front of my mom.

You just don't do that.

If he hadn't used the f-word, she would have believed him. She would have heard him out, and she would have believed him. She would have called Katie Catherine and me over right then and there, and she would have asked us if it was true.

And I would have stood right there in that driveway, and I would have lied.

Mom would have taken one look at my face and known I was lying, and she would have asked one more time, and I would have lied one more time, and she would have said, "Patricia Anne? You tell me the truth right now, or I'll…" and my bottom lip would have quivered so bad until I cried, and I would have fessed up. Right then and there, it would have been over. I would have returned the loot and said I was sorry and promised to never do it again. I'd have been grounded alright, and I would have begged my mom to "please—please—please don't tell Daddy. I'll do anything, just please don't tell Daddy." And she'd have been mad as hell at me, but then it would have all blown over.

I'm not saying he would have lived to see the day he was rocking on his front porch, bouncing a grandkid on his bony knee. He was a mean son of a bitch, and surely someone would have killed him by now.

But if he hadn't cussed in front of my mom, Ronnie Clark would have lived through the summer of 1976.

But he said *fuck* in front of my mother.

And you just don't do that.

1

April 1973

"Mommy?"

"Yes, darlin'?"

"When we move to our new house, will we still be on top of the world?"

"Yes, darlin'."

At five, my understanding of the earth and my place on it was based largely on the big blue National Geographic globe in the living room. And my understanding of the big blue globe was based largely on whatever my four older, wiser siblings taught me. If one of them learned about China in school that day, they would show me where China is. If they learned to count in Spanish, they would teach me to count in Spanish and show me where Spain is. Every time, I would ask, "And where are we?"

With one of my fingers on the new country, they would put my other finger on America, each state a different pastel color.

"OK, now where's Michigan?" they would ask.

"Right there."

Michigan is the easiest to find because it's shaped like a mitten. And each time I saw it, I took comfort in knowing we were on top of the world, where we wouldn't fall off.

At five, I knew just enough about gravity to know it could be your friend or your enemy, but I didn't understand how

5

people below the equator didn't fall off. There were some sleep-
less nights worrying about the people of Australia and Brazil
clinging on for dear life. My theory was that's why koala bears
hold on to trees and monkeys have prehensile tails.

So when my mom told us we were moving from our house
in Detroit to a farm in the country, my first concern was for our
safety, gravitywise.

Karen and Mary went to the globe.

"See the mitten?" Karen asked.

"Yeah," I responded.

"Don't say 'yeah,' dear," Mom corrected.

"See where we are now?" Mary asked, pointing to Detroit
with her pencil.

"Yeah—mm-hmm," I replied.

"We're moving to about...here," she said, pointing to the
unmarked space at the bottom of the mitten—the nondescript,
open frontier between Detroit and Chicago, just above where
Indiana and Ohio border each other. I was relieved to know we
wouldn't be losing much latitude.

If you grow up in Michigan, the most important lesson in
geography goes something like this:

1. Hold up your right hand, fingers together like you're
   swearing an oath.
2. This is Michigan.
3. Point to your hometown and say, "I'm from (insert
   hometown here)."

For the rest of your life, when you leave Michigan and someone asks where you're from, you'll say, "Michigan," reflexively
hold up your mitten, and point to your hometown. To help

non-Michiganders better understand, you'll follow that with the distance (in hours, not miles) and direction from Detroit. Kalamazoo: two hours due west of Detroit. Frankenmuth: an hour and a half north of Detroit.

Unless you're from Detroit. Heck, everyone knows where that is.

Catherine held up her right hand. "Trisha. Hold up your hand. Point to where we are. Where is Detroit?"

I pointed, proudly.

She took my finger and moved it about an inch west. "There. That's where we're going. That's Pittsford."

There it was. Right in my hand.

Dan, the oldest and only boy, pulled out Daddy's road atlas and spread it on the floor. "Here, dummy. This is where we're moving. The middle of nowhere."

"Daniel! It is not," Mom said. "You're going to love it there. You'll make new friends."

"There won't be any girls there."

"There will be girls there."

"Ugly ones," he said under his breath.

"Nice ones," Mom said. "Not like those fresh girls at your school."

"And cute boys?" Mary asked.

"You girls don't need to be thinking about boys, Mary Adrene," Mom said, looking over her glasses.

"Mom? Will there be horses?" asked Catherine.

"Yes, Katie Catherine. There are horses in Pittsford."

2

---•---

Nothing Bad Happens Here

Dan was wrong.

If Nowhere has a geographical dead center, Pittsford, Michigan isn't quite it. Pittsford is one of eight towns and villages that make up Hillsdale County, the southernmost point in the state. The region was settled by immigrants with three or more syllables in their names, like Vanarsdale, Davenport, and Trumbauer. Lured by fertile soil, fresh water, abundant timber, and game, all for $1.25 an acre, they traveled from New England to Detroit. Covered wagons then carried them west on the Sauk Trail—a prehistoric path originally cut by woolly mammoths, inured by Indians, and now known as highway US 12.

Even today, almost two hundred years after the first European set foot there, you can see the history in their faces, passed down through the generations of families who settled and stayed here. The dirt under their nails is the same rich soil that fed tribes and settlers alike, the earth that absorbed the spilled blood of outlaws, and the dust from streets of once-bustling railroad towns now long gone. Don't be surprised if you meet someone whose last name is also the name of a road or a landmark. And they're not even a snob about it.

Pittsford is small enough to be classified as a village, not even a town. At the end of its tree-lined main street, you'll find a bank, a bar, a store, a school, a gas station, and a post office. There's even a flashing light where highway M-34 cuts through town. It says, "You don't have to stop, but dammit, at least acknowledge there's something here."

The bank is robbed frequently because Pittsford doesn't have a police force. The bar and the gas station are never robbed because they're locally owned. The hardware store has creaky wooden floors and barrels full of nails, and every inch of every wall is covered with everything you could need but in no discernible order. Behind the counter is a weathered old man who, by god, knows where everything is and what it's for, and he could, by god, fix anything.

Scattered over the county are a few small factories and tool and die shops that supply Detroit, but this is farm country. Right smack in the center of Pittsford stands the feed mill, a whitewashed behemoth of a barn with a rusty green roof, and a pair of shiny tin silos. The south side has loading docks where you can dump your harvest in the morning and come back that afternoon to load up the bags of your freshly milled corn.

When people say "It's a good place to raise a family," they're talking about places like Pittsford. Nothing bad ever happens there. Fields of corn, soy, and alfalfa in every direction, with soil so dark and rich it's like walking on warm chocolate cake. Dairy farms with pastures of fat Holsteins grazing in the sun, swishing away flies with their long white tails. The crack of a bat at the church softball game can be heard a mile away.

This would become my hometown. Witness to my life, setting to my story.

And nothing bad happens here.

3

Until It Wasn't

It was precisely because nothing bad happens there that Dewey and Betty uprooted their lives and moved their brood to Pittsford. They were fugitives of a sort, leaving bad behind.

Both native Detroiters and neither more than two generations from the boat, my folks found each other despite coming from opposite sides of the tracks. My dad's family never lived in the same place for more than two years. He and his four siblings often shared a room in whatever house they could afford to rent. Mom grew up in an unassuming bungalow on a tree-lined street, practicing her majorette baton moves in the backyard. She and her brother had their own bedrooms with wallpaper and matching bedcovers.

Mom starred in school plays and graduated at the top of her class. Daddy dropped out of eighth grade to work odd jobs, supporting his family through the Great Depression.

During Prohibition, my mother's father—a successful electrical engineer—made extra money as a bootlegger for the mafia, running rum across the river from Canada in his Chris-Craft. My dad and his father carted blocks of ice to blind pig parties, where they likely served that rum in the tony parts of town or the underground boxing matches in the seedier parts.

At seventeen, Dewey lied about his age to join the navy and fight in the war because he "didn't want to miss out."

Betty was much younger but fondly recalls selling war bonds door-to-door in her neighborhood and growing radishes and corn in the family's victory garden.

Postwar Detroit was a boomtown, flush with jobs and opportunity, raising all boats with the tide. When he got home from the war, Dewey followed his dad into the trucking business, hauling parts for the growing auto industry and quickly lifting their family from poverty to the working class.

By the time my parents met, Dewey was established as a long-haul trucker for a small but well-connected company. They weren't rich but made enough to afford a modest home on a quiet street, a car in the driveway, and the occasional Sunday picnic on Belle Isle. Over time, they did well enough to buy two rigs of their own and hired on drivers.

Suffice it to say, Detroit was good to them.

Until it wasn't.

By 1970, the boom had busted. After a decade of hemorrhaging people and jobs, the thriving city they knew was no more. The good drained out of Detroit like dirty bathwater from a tub. On a cold February night in 1973, that dirty water spilled into our home.

Daddy was on a run, and the older kids were at the neighbors' for a sleepover, so it was just my mom and me. We were watching TV when there was a knock at the door. When Mom opened it, a bloodied man with a gun forced his way in, pushing her to the floor. She stood up and motioned for me to get down where he couldn't see me.

"Who else is here?" he demanded, pointing the gun around to the other rooms.

"No one," Mom replied calmly. "My husband is a truck driver."

He stood listening for a minute, eyes shifting left and right. Using the barrel of the gun to rub his cheek as if he were contemplating. His eyes closed, and his head rolled back slowly until his mouth was agape. Mom turned around to me, put her finger to her lips and mouthed, "Stay." She tiptoed toward him, reaching for the gun.

His head popped forward, and he gasped and choked, spraying dark blood on Mom's face and chest.

"Okay," he muttered. "Get in the kitchen where I can see you. Both of you."

Mom took my hand and sat me at the table. Before she could sit, he barked, "You got any tuna fish? How 'bout you make me a tuna fish sandwich, ma'am?"

"Yes, of course," she replied. "I…I thought you looked hungry."

She sat him down with a plate of food and a glass of milk, talking gently until he put his gun on the table. As he ate, she noticed blood dripping from his head, down his neck and soaking the white T-shirt under his jacket.

"Let me clean up that cut on your head while you eat. I'm a nurse," she lied.

He grunted and continued eating. When he took a drink, the blood from his mouth sloshed back into the glass, turning his milk pink.

"Trisha, darlin', don't stare," Mom said. "Go to the bathroom and bring me a towel."

I came back with the towel from the rack.

"Not that one, dear. Those were a wedding present," she said. "Get a plain one."

As she wiped the blood on his head, she noticed a piece of his skull hanging down. Gently, she put it back in place and wrapped his whole head like a turban. Weak from loss of blood, he nodded off on his plate. Soon after, the police knocked on the door. Our visitor had fled the scene of an armed robbery, where he had been shot, and crashed his car nearby. They followed his tracks and a trail of blood in the snow, right to our door.

Family folklore has it that Betty left us kids with a neighbor the next day and drove west on US 12 for hours until she could no longer see concrete or a building taller than three stories. She found the Byrne farm: forty acres in the shape of an American flag. The blue box of stars is a small forest, hemmed in by a deep creek. The stripes are tillable acres, the house and barn sitting bottom center.

And nothing bad happens here.

4

Real to Me

When I tell you I grew up on a farm, don't believe me. I'm lying. It wasn't a real farm.

It was real in that it *had been* a real farm, established in 1852 by the Byrne family. Three generations grew alfalfa and built a small dairy operation. It was real in that it had a big white farmhouse, a bigger red barn, and a silo.

But it ceased being a real farm when the city slickers moved in. Despite having zero experience, Mom wasted no time populating the farm with animals. At first it was just poultry she could buy at the farm supply store. Boxes of tiny baby chicks and ducklings sat on the dining room table, kept warm with a bright light bulb. Us kids loved holding them and letting them nestle in the crooks of our necks. Soon we had flocks of chickens and ducks roaming everywhere, making nests and leaving eggs anywhere. As the youngest, it was my job to find and collect them. We didn't know enough to separate the roosters, so it wasn't unusual to pick up fertilized eggs. Making an omelet became a gamble.

By the end of the summer, we were going to the Saturday livestock auctions at the county fairgrounds. On more than one occasion, Mom had to bring smaller livestock, like calves, home in the Buick. We would pile in the back seat and hold the calf on our laps, giggling and hoping it wouldn't crap on us.

By fall that first year, we had six pigs and two cows, a mother and calf we named Sweetums and Cuddles. They were an Angus-Holstein cross, black with white faces and bellies, cute white curls on their foreheads and at the ends of their tails.

Bertha the pig gave us a surprise one hot August night. She had been pacing and circling in her pen, rooting all the straw to one corner. We found her that night, lying on her side, breathing heavily with a swollen belly. We ran to fetch Mom, and she called Doc Callaghan.

"Sounds like she's ready to farrow, Missus White," he said. "She's having babies. Don't you worry now, she'll do all the work. Unless this is her first time, then she might get scared." He walked her through what to do and said to call if we had any problems.

Mom and I climbed into the pen; I sat by Bertha's head, stroking her face and ears, and Mom knelt at the business end. When the piglets started coming, Bertha huffed and stretched her back legs. All but one came out on its own. Mom had to reach in and pull it out by its back feet. Over the course of an hour, she gave birth to six piglets, five breathing and one dead.

They began moving around immediately, covered with blood and goo. Mom wiped them off, and it was my job to place them on a teat and help them latch. Mom had a good laugh when one wriggled his way back down to Bertha's nethers and I said, "Mommy, this one's trying to get back in!"

Daddy would come home from two-week runs to find yet more and more animals filling up the barn and paddock. "Betty Lou!" he'd holler. "What the hell are you thinking? Who's gonna take care of all these goddamn animals?"

"The kids, dear. The chores will be good for them. Keep them out of trouble and teach them responsibility."

It wasn't a real farm, but it was real to me. I was just a kid and never knew any different. It wasn't until I was an adult that I realized it was just a glorified petting zoo.

5

Not the Romantic Idea

Catherine came out of the womb loving animals. Her first word was *dog*, and for at least a year after that, she talked exclusively to animals and only in her special language. No "mama" or "dada" for her. She would follow Timothy the cat around the house, jabbering like she was expecting him to talk back. On more than one occasion, she climbed out of her crib and curled up on the floor with our dogs, Sarge and McKeever. Mom would find her there in the morning, sound asleep.

But it was horses that lit her up. Yeah, I know people think all girls are horse crazy, but that's bullshit. Catherine wasn't into unicorns or little pink ponies. She didn't dream of Disneyfied stallions galloping across a meadow. To her, every horse, no matter how ordinary, was extraordinary. She read every book and saw every movie—*National Velvet, Black Beauty, Misty of Chincoteague*. If a horse was hurt in a Western movie, she would cry until Mom explained that the horse was only acting, just like the people. She sketched horses in notebooks and the margins of her Bible. She built horses out of couch cushions. She memorized every anatomical part of a horse—withers, fetlock, croup, hock. And every breed—Arabian, Thoroughbred, Morgan. My favorite was always the Appaloosa.

She would steal plastic margarine bowls from the kitchen and tie them to her feet so she could have hooves and make a clip-clop sound. While Karen and Mary were playing with dolls, Catherine was galloping around the yard with a scarf tucked down the back of her pants as a makeshift tail. She taught herself to whinny and got so good at it, horses would whinny back. Just for laughs, we would get her to do it in a crowd or at the mall, making everyone turn to look for the horse.

When we went to the Saturday livestock auctions at the fairground, Catherine and I would make a beeline for the horse barns, where they stabled the trotters. We lurked up and down the rows, hoping they would stick their heads out so we could pet their faces and feed them peppermints from her pocket. Do you know how to spot a girl who really loves horses—and not just the romantic idea of them? When she buries her face in a sweaty horse's mane and inhales deeply, just to fill her lungs with the smell.

6

Just Good Business

Surrounded on all sides by real farmers, we were a constant source of amusement for the neighbors. Mostly the Kjellberg family, a farming dynasty in Hillsdale County. Grandma and Grandpa Kjellberg's farm is over on Bacon Road, Big Darryl and Vicky are down the road, and cousins Jack Junior and Loretta lived just around the corner from us. They would drive by in their dusty pickups and wave, chuckling. I'm sure it was like watching a live-action *Green Acres*.

Don't get me wrong—they were also endlessly kind and generous. If there's a college course on tribalism and xenophobia in rural America, I'd love to know what they have to say about this phenomenon. Even though we were totally out of our element, they were always ready with the right answers and the right tools. They could fix anything, pull any vehicle out of the ditch, and heal any animal. If they couldn't do it, they knew someone who could. They kept us in groceries during the blizzard of '78, driving to town on their snowmobiles while we were snowed in for weeks. If ever they were condescending, we probably had that coming.

Big Darryl and Vicky lived closest and had a passel of kids just like us. But while we had lots of girls and one boy, they had lots of boys and one girl. Grown-ups would joke about it, telling my dad he had better lock the doors. As a kid,

I didn't know what they meant, but I assumed us girls needed to be locked in because we were dangerous in numbers.

Mom was determined to become the best blue-ribbon farmwife she could be. She seemed unaware that this is not something you can learn or achieve any more than you can learn to become a giraffe. You can't even marry into it. If you weren't born and raised on a farm, you'll never be a real farmer. On some level, you'll always be an outsider. A poser.

Betty tried to physically morph into a farmwife but failed miserably. She stopped dyeing her hair and let the salt and pepper take over. Eventually, reluctantly, she stopped wearing full makeup to get groceries in town, all the while lamenting the good ol' days when "ladies dressed properly to go out of the house." But she never wore jeans or heavy fabrics, only fitted polyester pants and feminine blousy tops. All her shoes—even her rain boots—had at least a one-inch heel. While farmwives had brown arms, freckled cheeks, and burned noses from spending hours in the sun, she kept her milky alabaster complexion under wide-brimmed hats. Farmwives had calluses on their hands and dirt under their nails. Betty wore gloves religiously.

She was always going to fail at fitting in. Even if she could have adopted their mannerisms or worn their clothing like a costume, she was simply a different species. Her features were angular like a shark: high cheekbones and brows, a long jawline, a deep widow's peak. Her eyes weren't extraordinary except that there was something broken in them. The blue was cracked with dark brown, like a cobalt plate left to shatter in the cold. Mercifully, she rarely made eye contact.

She was kind but not warm. Pretty but not beautiful. She seemed happy but not content. She smiled but didn't show her teeth. She was popular but not particularly liked. When I was little, I assumed I would understand her when I was older. Humans look for patterns; we build archetypes to interpret others. But when you're finished reading this book, you won't know her any better than I do. I've had a front-row seat my whole life, and I still don't understand her. There's a reason I waited until she was in the ground before I told this story.

How could this interloper get them to like her, trust her, and teach her? If she was to succeed, she needed the blessings of the locals, especially the farmwives. Looking back on it, I see it as her four-part ingratiation plan, a campaign to build a century of family farm roots and goodwill in twelve months or less.

First, let's meet the neighbors and feed them well. That first summer, Daddy built his truck garage, a large red pole barn big enough to park an eighteen-wheeler. Before he had a chance to move in, Mom used the space to host a huge picnic to thank the neighbors for their hospitality. She must have borrowed every folding table in a five-mile radius and set up one very long picnic table, complete with the classic red-and-white checkered tablecloth.

Did she pull out the barbeque and serve hot dogs and coleslaw at her picnic? Nope. Not Betty Lou. She served her signature dish: real Italian spaghetti. Did she use a couple jars of Chef Boyardee? How dare you.

Her own mother was a terrible cook, and she wasn't much better, but she did learn to make this one thing very well. Our neighbor lady in Detroit, Mrs. Bernardi, was an old-school right-off-the-boat Sicilian widow. During the long weeks with Daddy on the road, Mom would spend time at Mrs. Bernardi's kitchen table, talking about the good old days and commiserating about husbands gone away. That's where Mom learned to make "the sauce."

The first ingredient is time. A minimum of three days in the kitchen, chopping, marinating, simmering, stirring, testing, watching, and waiting. Kids were recruited to stir to keep the sauce from sticking to the bottom of a twenty-quart stockpot so tall we had to stand on a chair to reach it. Certain ingredients like onions and green peppers must be fresh, and others must be canned, but only a particular brand of this and another brand for that. Hunt's tomato paste but not their puree because it was too acidic. She could work with frozen meats for the sauce, but they had to be thawed slowly in the fridge and braised only in a properly seasoned cast-iron pan before joining the rest in the pot. Don't ask me about the spices she used. Hell, I don't think she knew what witches' brew went into it. And finally, only Mueller's vermicelli. Never spaghetti noodles. So pedestrian.

At the picnic, she personally plated each person's spaghetti while the kids poured sweet tea and passed around Parmesan cheese—or "stinky cheese," as we called it. My job was to deliver thick slices of fresh-baked Italian bread, crusty on the outside and fleshy soft on the inside.

Daddy sat at the head of the table. A man of few words, he smiled and laughed, listening intently to all the guests' stories. He had a gift for making anyone feel interesting and important. He almost never talked about himself. If you sat with him long enough, you could eventually get a story or two out of him, but he never offered it up easily. And when the conversation ended, you really liked him even though you didn't know much about him.

If I saw someone like him today, I would assume he was in the witness protection program. He was a truck driver, yes, but he was no grease monkey. More like a movie star with a Class C driver's license. Thick wavy hair, dimples for days, perfect teeth, and blue eyes. A little Dean Martin and a little James Dean, he had that slick 1950s Rat Pack style in a blue-collar uniform. My dad was the guy Patsy Cline and Doris Day wrote all those songs about. Fall to pieces indeed.

None of this was lost on the neighbor ladies. Eyelashes were batted, fingers twirled locks of hair, and voices were a bit breathier when they talked to him. Daddy wasn't a flirt; he was just so goddamned charming, he had that effect on women.

Nurses, waitresses, grocery clerks, post office ladies, teachers—you name it, they all went gaga over Daddy. He was blissfully unaware; when we teased him about it, he would just shake his head and laugh, insisting we were crazy.

He charmed their husbands too. He was a man's man with a strong handshake. He smelled like cigarettes and diesel with a hint of aftershave. Even the ones who didn't want to like him because he was a city slicker had to come around after spending the afternoon with him.

Once everyone had their fill of mom's spaghetti, the men eventually loosened their belts and pushed their full bellies away from the table. As men do, they flocked to a nearby vehicle and looked under the hood for hours. The wives complimented Mom's sauce and grilled her for the recipe as they helped clear the table.

Betty had done it. In one day and fourteen quarts of spaghetti sauce, she forged bonds and fast-tracked friendships.

The second plank of Mom's ingratiation campaign was visiting our new school, meeting the staff, and demonstrating her superior parenting skills by encouraging all teachers, principals, and coaches to feel free to beat her children if they ever got out of line—and then call her so she could beat them again when they got home. Yes, she did that.

In Detroit, we had all gone to different schools—the older three were in junior high, Catherine was in elementary, and I was in preschool—and each one of them was bigger than our new school. In the tiny village of Pittsford, all grades go to one school, an L-shaped building with elementary students on one side and middle and high school on the other. It's as if you go in at one end for kindergarten, proceed through grades like you're being digested by a snake, and come out the other end when you graduate.

But now, we were the new kids—the new kids in a school where classes are small and teachers know every student. They know your history, your coaches, friends, siblings, parents, and where you live. We were the new kids in a place where almost no one moved to or away from, so we were a novelty—and there was no place to hide from our mistakes, as small as they might seem.

Betty wasn't taking chances on her kids screwing this up.

Third, get the family in church. Mom was raised Episcopalian, and Daddy's family was Lutheran, so the denomination didn't matter; just pick the biggest one. Reassure everyone in town that we are good, God-fearing people raising their kids to be good, God-fearing Christians. We didn't attend church in Detroit, so I didn't really know what to expect except what I saw in movies and on TV. Should I kneel? Do I touch my forehead? Will I be fed a cracker?

Fourth and finally, ding-dong! Mom became an Avon lady. In no time, she was winning all the sales awards and President's Club, regional this and statewide that. She won cash and prizes like a VCR, a microwave, and even a lawn mower. Sometimes she would take me along to meetings. She would be dressed smartly, hair up, wearing Avon's latest eye shadow or necklace. When she walked across the room, the other women shushed and stared. Was it hate I saw in their eyes? Or envy? Either way, I admired my mom for that.

Betty wasn't in it to make money, and she wasn't in it to make friends either. She did it for the sport. I learned years later that she was tops in sales because she sold everything at cost, i.e., steep discounts. Once she conquered her own territory, she started siphoning off customers from other ladies' territories. Who could blame customers for dropping Janet or Evelyn when they could get their favorites for half price from Betty? It wasn't against the rules if the customers came to you. This cutthroat sales strategy won her many prizes but sure didn't win her any friends among fellow Avon ladies.

Say what you will, she was brilliant. Think about it—the Avon lady gains access to your home, your family, your life. She knows everything about you. She's privy to personal information like what soap you use because your kid has an allergy, what you use to cover those bags under your eyes, and how much cologne your husband uses. Financial information like how much you can afford. Do you pay with cash or check?

And while she plies you with discounts and free samples, you dish about the who's who of Hillsdale County, the muckety-mucks and the have-nots. You give her the dirt on who's divorced and why, who was a slut in high school, who dyes her hair or drinks too much at Thursday night bowling league, which farms are in trouble with the bank, and whose husbands beat them and why. The information she gleaned from one could be bartered for favor from another.

Proverbs says the godless destroy their neighbors with their mouths. Mom says that's just good business.

7

Summer 1973

"I'm taking the girls school shopping tomorrow," Mom said at supper.

"Hmmph," Daddy grumbled, sawing at a pork chop.

"Krogers has that sweet corn you like on special, six for a dollar," Mom said. "Do you want me to pick up some more while I'm in town?"

In this part of Michigan, people add an *s* to the names of most stores and businesses. Not a possessive *s* or a plural *s*, just an *s*. So Kroger becomes Krogers, Meijer becomes Meijers. Your Christmas presents are on layaway at Kmarts, your dad works at Fords.

"Have any of you kids met the new neighbors?" she asked. "The ones who moved in down at the Nafziger's place?"

"Nope," Mary said.

"Don't say 'nope,'" Mom said.

"No," Mary said.

"No what?" Daddy said.

"No, ma'am," Mary said.

"Well maybe we'll stop by on the way back from town tomorrow," Mom said.

"Can't you give them time to settle in, Betty Lou?" Daddy asked.

"They've been there almost a whole week. I don't want them to think we're unneighborly."

"Hmmph," Daddy grunted.

Neighborly? Mom could smell a new customer within a twenty-five-mile radius. So when a new family moved in, she was on them like a duck on a June bug. We were just happy to no longer be the "new" family.

As we pulled in the driveway, nothing seemed out of place as you would expect for a family that had recently moved in. No boxes on the lawn, no bikes or toys.

"OK, girls, sit tight and I'll be right back," Mom said, checking her lipstick in the rearview mirror. "I'm just going to drop off these catalogs."

All four of us were holding our back-to-school shopping haul on our laps. My bag didn't have clothes because all my back-to-school clothes would be hand-me-downs, one of the perks of having three older sisters. But I was excited to get school supplies, including pencils and lined paper like the big kids used.

Before Mom could knock, the lady of the house was at the door. She was short and thick with a tan that failed to cover the dark crescents under her sunken eyes. She was wearing a macramé halter top and cutoff jean shorts. Her shade of blonde was what my mother would call "dishwater."

"Yeah?" she said through the screen door.

"Well hello, neighbor!" Mom said. "I'm Betty. Betty White. We live right up the road there, on the other side of Lamb Road."

"Oh yeah, hi," she said. "Sorry, I, uh, I'm really b—"

"I'm sure you're very busy settling in," Mom said with a comforting smile. "I just wanted to say hello and drop off these catalogs. I sell Avon, and I can get you a great discount on anything you and your family need. Do you have children?"

As she pushed open the screen door to take the catalogs, two boys ran past her, pushing her back against the doorjamb and nearly running Mom over.

"Goddammit, boys!" she yelled after them. "Watch where the hell y'all are going! Goddamned animals."

They fell in a heap in the yard, laughing and punching each other, yelling "Faggot!" and "You're the faggot!"

"I'm so sorry. Those boys... They just don't have no manners." She laughed nervously. "Like a couple of wild Indians."

"I can see that," Mom said. "Maybe their father can talk to them and work on that."

The woman looked past Mom, stepping back and letting the screen door close without taking the catalogs. Her brown eyes caught the daylight, and her pupils constricted to pinpoints.

"Boys will be boys, won't they now?" a voice grumbled behind Mom.

Leaning against our car, wiping his greasy hands on his shirt, he might have fancied himself a Marlboro man, but he smoked Pall Malls, a squished soft pack tucked in his shirt pocket. His boots were too fancy, and his hat was too big, casting a shadow that cut across his face. He would have been over six feet tall if he stood up straight. At each side of him perched identical Doberman pinschers, their docked ears alert.

"Oh!" Mom startled. "Oh my, you scared me," she said, clutching her chest.

"Sorry, ma'am. So, what can we do for you ladies today?" he asked, leering down at us in the car.

"Oh, I came by to say hello and introduce myself," Mom said. "I'm Betty. Betty White. We live just up the road, right up Culbert there on the other side of Lamb Road."

"Is that right?" he asked, stepping toward Mom. He barked a command, and the Dobermans sat at attention right in front of our car, never taking their eyes off us. A thick Southern drawl flattened his vowels—*right* sounded like *rot*.

"Yes, we're the ones on the north side of the road there. With the big red pole barn. That's my husband Dewey's garage. We have a trucking company."

"Is that right?" He was chewing on a toothpick and sucking his teeth.

"Yes. Well, and what do you do, Mister—uh, I'm sorry, what is your name?"

He flicked a match head with his thumbnail and lit a Pall Mall.

"Clark. Ronnie Clark."

8

Don't Worry, Girls

"Pleased to meet you, Ron," Mom said. "And I didn't catch your name?" she added, turning back to the screen door.

Mrs. Clark was still frozen, exactly as she was before, her eyes fixed on Ronnie Clark.

"That there's Angie," he said. "My wife."

"How do you do?" Mom said.

"Boys!" Ronnie Clark barked, tilting his hat back on his head.

The boys started slinking away, trying to make their way to the other side of the house.

"Goddammit, if I have to catch you, it'll be a sight worse," Ronnie Clark shouted.

The boys slowed to a halt, turned to look at each other, then trotted obediently right to him. He buried his hands in their greasy hair and yanked them down to the ground at his feet. They yelped but didn't cry out.

With one fancy boot, he slowly stepped down onto the fingers of boy number one. With the other fancy boot, he stepped on the back of boy number two's neck. He trained his gaze on my mom and puffed his Pall Mall. "You boys gonna say sorry to Miz White."

"Ron, please. Really. They're just a little rambunctious," Mom said. "And it's…uh…Mrs. White," she corrected.

"They're ill-mannered little Injuns. Like you said. They need their daddy to learn 'em some manners. Like you said." He leaned more weight on the boys. They winced but still didn't cry. "Ain't that what you said?"

"Well, I…I just meant…" Mom said.

"I know what you meant." He stepped off the boys and kicked boy number one in the ribs. "Get up. And say you're sorry to *Missus* White."

They stood up and said "Sorry Miz White" in unison.

"Now get the hell outa here, dipshits," he said, smacking their heads. They ran behind the house. "You have any boys, *Missus* White?" Ronnie Clark asked, snuffing out his cigarette.

"Yes, Dan. He's our oldest. He's seventeen."

"He a good boy, Missus White? Did his daddy teach him manners?"

"Oh yes. He's a good—"

"He want a job, Missus White?"

"Oh, well, he works with his father, so—"

"Got a lot of brush around here needs clearing, and those two retards can't be trusted with a power tool. Got fence to be fixed, stalls to be cleaned. Those two are about as useful as tits on a boar hog. They ain't right in the head. Runs in their momma's side of the family," he said, looking at Angie. "Ain't that right, sugar?"

"Well, Angie, as I was saying, I'm an Avon representative, and so I can get you all the things you need for your family, and I can get them for you at a discount," Mom said as she held out the catalogs toward the screen door again.

Angie pushed the door open, cautiously reaching around to take the catalogs.

Ronnie Clark pounced forward, snatching the catalogs out of Angie's hand. "Hold up, now. We won't be needin' any of your fancy Avon." He handed the catalogs back to my mom.

"It's not really fancy. Well, I mean, some of it is. There's the Moonwind collection, but most of it is just everyday things, soaps and shampoos, you know? And even some nice shaving things and colognes for you." The edges of her mouth curled up.

He stepped closer and pushed the catalogs back to her.

Undaunted, she opened one and flipped through it. "See, here." She held it up for him to see. "This one here is Wild Country. It's for cowboys like you." She smiled.

"Is that right?" He smiled back, sauntering to our car.

"Dewey—that's my husband—he likes Today's Man. Oh, it just smells so good on him. So masculine. When he wears that, I can barely keep my hands off him." She blushed.

"Is that right?" Ronnie Clark stepped to the side of our car. With his back to Mom, he leaned on the car window, leering in at us. On the back of his hand was a tattoo of a Kewpie doll with "Daddy's Little Girl" inked in boxy script.

"Dewey's a lucky man, Missus White," he said, looking from one girl to the other, up the torsos and down the legs. He took a deep breath, smelling us like prey. "You gave him all these daughters," he said. "Alls I got were those damn boys. Good-for-nuthin' shit heels."

Ronnie Clark had one brown eye and one lazy pale-blue eye. The brown eye shifted quickly, and the pale-blue one would wander aimlessly, then eventually catch up. From the side, he seemed handsome and even kind. But when he looked straight at you, he downright scared the shit out of you. With his back to the house, his one good eye staring straight at Karen, he ran his tongue slowly over his top lip and winked, flashing a shiny gold tooth.

"Don't worry, girls," he whispered. "*I ain't dangerous.*"

"Yes, well…" Mom said nervously. She rifled through her bag and pulled out a generous handful of free samples. "Angie, I'm gonna leave you these free samples. Go ahead and try them out, see what you think. Our phone number is right there on the back." Making her way toward the car, Mom said, "All my customers just love Skin So Soft. You might like that too, Mr. Clark. It's good for cleaning grease off your hands. And it'll keep the mosquitoes off you too. It's a miracle product."

"Miracle, huh?" he said. "We ain't yer simpleminded yokels like these hicks and hayseeds around here, Miz White. You gonna have to sell your snake oil somewheres else."

"Yes, well…" Mom said, stepping gingerly around the Dobermans.

"Here!" he barked, and the dogs ran to him. "See that? Only ones around here who listen. These dogs won't take a shit without being told."

"Oh…well…that's…" Mom said, still moving to the car.

"Miz White, do you know these dogs can be eating out of your hand one second and eating your throat the next, by my command?" he said, pounding his chest. "And you know what else?" He glanced at Angie. "I'm the only one knows that command."

"Well, we'll be going now. It was so nice to meet you, Angie. And you, Ron. If you change your mind about the Skin So Soft, you just let me know."

9

Fall 1973

"Mrs. White? We need to talk about Trisha."

This was a phone call Betty would get many times over the years. The second time was during my first week of kindergarten at Pittsford school. Mrs. Baumgartner, my teacher, called to tell my mom I would not stay in my seat and was "visiting the other children at their desks."

"My Trisha?" Mom said. "That doesn't sound like my Trisha. She's a smart girl."

"Oh, it's not that, Mrs. White," said Mrs. Baumgartner. "Trisha's very good with her skills. She knows her alphabet and is reading and writing at a higher grade level. We just can't get her to stay put."

Let me back up a minute and tell you about the first time Mom got that call.

When Mom asked me what I wanted for my third birthday, I told her I wanted to learn to write my name. Painfully aware that everyone was older and wiser, I resented them for leaving me every day, going to a magical place called school where smart people taught them new things. So after supper and birthday cake, we sat down at the coffee table, and Mom taught me how to write both my given name, Patricia Anne, and my everyday name, Trisha. She also taught me our address and phone number, in case I ever got lost.

When I was four, Mom saw an ad in the newspaper for a preschool and immediately signed me up. Let me paint the picture: The perfunctory first-day-of-school picture shows the yellow bus approaching in the background, and there's me in a big smile and a little dress, knee socks, and sneakers, holding a little red purse and a notebook. My pageboy haircut was pinned back with a barrette. The days of being the baby left behind with Mommy every day while the big kids got to go to school were over. I had arrived.

"Mrs. White? We need to talk about Trisha."

The call came that night after what I'm sure was a very confused group of teachers and administrators had assembled to discuss how to handle this unprecedented situation. You see, the advertisement read "Do you have a *special* child? ABC Preschool is for you."

"Well…Trisha doesn't belong in this school," they explained. "She isn't, ahem, *special.*"

"I beg your pardon, of course she is!" Mom exclaimed. "She's very special! She's already reading and writing!"

They explained that the contemporary meaning of the word *special* in this context was a euphemism for mentally challenged children. After recovering from embarrassment, Mom explained that I had been looking forward to this for weeks, so excited to finally be going to school like the big kids.

"She was so happy when she got home today," Mom said. "She hasn't shut up about it. How am I going to tell her she can't go back to school tomorrow? She's four. She doesn't understand that she's different from them. They're just kids."

Mom was able to work out a deal with them: I could continue to go to preschool, and no one would let on that I was different. The teachers were happy to have an enthusiastic little helper, and I was thrilled to be going to school.

Mom neglected to tell me this story until I was well into my twenties. But when I heard it, the kindergarten trouble finally made sense. My "job" in preschool was to help the other kids, so that's what I thought school was. When I started kindergarten, I assumed I was supposed to help the other kids, so I went from desk to desk, *helping*. It wouldn't be the last time my good intentions had consequences.

10

Thanksgiving 1973

Click. "Good morning, Wildcats. Are we all excited for Thanksgiving lunch today? I heard that our lovely cafeteria ladies have prepared turkey, stuffing, and mashed potatoes for us. Nutritious and delicious, OK? And then we have our Thanksgiving assembly this afternoon." Click.

"Calm down, kids, calm down," Mrs. Baumgartner said. Principal Dietrich's PA announcements always unleashed a round of snickers and comments. This being the day before Thanksgiving break, we were already bubbling with excitement. Just as she was getting us back under control...

Click. "Aaand can I get all the White kids to the high school principal's office? That's Dan, Karen, Mary, Catherine, and Trisha. Your mom is here...The cows are out again." Click.

Now the entire school erupted in laughter and jeers, so loud they echoed up and down the halls.
"Mooooo! Mooooo!"
"Mommy! Mommy! Your mommy is here!"
"Better go catch those cows!"

51

This scene would play out several times during our time at Pittsford school, and we quickly learned to be good sports about it. Partly because in a big family, you need thick skin and a sharp tongue to survive when sarcasm is the language of love. And partly because it only happened to us; no one else's cows got loose. Other kids were real farmers, with real fences and gates. They had live-stock with numbered ear tags. We had pet cows with names like Sweetums and Cuddles. And birthdays and background stories. And favorite snacks and places to be scratched.

Luckily, my older siblings were already popular in school. How could they not be? They were attractive, athletic, and talented. Dan was tall and skinny; the basketball and track coaches saw him coming a mile away. Karen and Mary were both on student council and the cheerleading squad. In a small school like ours, that made them quasi celebrities. My best friend, Becky Lynn Grosvenor, and I loved to watch them from the bleachers and do the cheers with them. But I really loved to see the other kids' faces light up when they saw my sisters. Everyone knew their names and knew I was their little sister. Sometimes my class would be lined up outside the cafeteria after lunch when the big kids were piling in. If I saw one of my siblings, I would call out their name like paparazzi, waving to try to get them to wave back. I was too little to be popular, but I was popular adjacent.

Catching the cows was always the same. Mom would drive us around until we found them, usually grazing in someone else's field or lawn. We would try to round them up, and they would take off, loping around, tossing their hips in defiance. For a moment, they pretended to be wild until one of us ran to fetch a bucket of grain. Sweetums would come trotting, and the rest followed right along.

This time, they managed to get a bit farther away and deeper from the road.

This time, their defiant little romp went on for a mile or so.

This time, they made it all the way to Ronnie Clark's before we could get back with the bucket of grain.

"Well lookee here," Ronnie Clark huffed. "The city kids done lost their cows, now ain't they?" He was leaning up against his pickup, a rifle by his side and a Pall Mall dangling on his lip. Johnny Cash was singing "I Walk the Line" on the radio.

"Sorry, Mr. Clark," Dan said. "They found a soft spot in the fence, but we'll fix it. We'll get 'em out of here right away."

"You're sorry alright. Gonna be a might sorrier if these god-damned cows tear up my land." Picking up the rifle and pointing it at Sweetums, he said, "I do like a good steak." He pretended to cock the rifle and whispered, "Bang!"

I walk the line...

Mary had the bucket, leading the herd past him down the driveway to the road, the rest of us shooing from behind. He tipped his hat to the back of his head and stepped in front of her, making her sidestep around him, sliding against his truck.

"Yes, ma'am, these are some pretty little heifers." He ran his hand down the cows' backs as they walked past him, keeping his eyes trained on the girls. "Growin' up and out in all the right places," he hissed, licking his gold tooth.

I walk the line...

———•———

By the time we got the cows home, Grandma had arrived at the farm for Thanksgiving.

Now, I'm gonna need you to scratch your mental picture of a typical grandmother. Grandma was six feet tall. Svelte. Yes, she had gray hair and bejeweled horn-rimmed glasses, but she was the outdoorsy type. Utilitarian. She wore flannel, wool, and always pants—or "slacks," as she called them. She kept her hair short but not manly and drank her coffee from a red plaid thermos. Old black-and-white photos show her smiling and holding up a big fish on their Chris-Craft boat (yes, that same boat Grandpa used for bootlegging), skinning rabbits, and filleting the day's catch.

In a word, she was very Hemingway.

Grandma was first-generation American, raised by grateful immigrants who fled wars, domestic violence, and indentured servitude. Born in the states, she was actually conceived in occupied Alsace-Lorraine shortly before the First World War. Her mother escaped, but her father never made it out. He was a lumberjack, killed by a falling tree just days before he was to leave. Family folklore has it that the tree hit him on the head, and Grandma was born with a pink scar on her forehead.

Some years, we went to her place for Thanksgiving, a small cottage up north on Lake Huron in the part of the Michigan mitten called "the Thumb." She and Grandpa had built the cottage themselves in the 1950s when "up north" was still wild, cheap, and sparsely populated. Over time, it slowly built up around them, but it was always a treat to visit in the summer. We could swim in the lake and pick up shells and rocks on the beach all day, then crash on the sleeping porch and let the waves put us to sleep at night.

Grandma was old school. Old world. She did not tolerate ill-mannered children; no mischief, no back talk. She kept her cottage neat as a pin and had strict house rules. No shoes, no sand, no wet towels on the floor, no wet butts on the furniture. It's not that Grandma didn't bake cookies—she did. But they weren't for us.

On a road trip to the Mackinac Bridge shortly after Grandpa died, my shoe came untied while we were walking in a park. Mom wasn't around to help me, so I went to Grandma and stepped my little red shoe out in front of her.

"What?" she asked.

"My shoe," I answered.

"So? So tie it."

"I don't know how."

"What?! You don't…How old are you?"

"I'm three."

"You're not a baby, you should be able to tie your own shoe."

We sat right there, and she taught me how to tie my shoe—make a rabbit ear, loop around, push the other ear through, and pull them tight. Every time I did it wrong, she untied it and made me do it again, then a few more times for good measure.

"Daddy! Lookit!" I squealed, proudly untying and tying my shoe.

"How about that," he said with a smile, his pat response of approval.

———————•———————

When Mom learned that some of her kids' friends were, how shall I say, "less fortunate," she insisted they were invited to Thanksgiving supper. Sometimes "less fortunate" meant poor, but mostly it just meant their family didn't observe Thanksgiving by preparing a twenty-eight-pound turkey, stuffing, mashed potatoes and corn bread from scratch, two dozen deviled eggs, four desserts, and enough potato salad to fill a compact car. Either way, they were welcome at our table, as well as the occasional neighbor or Avon customer who stopped by just for the spectacle.

After supper, the house turned into a bit of a three-ring circus. With full bellies pushing waistbands to their limits and ice clinking in empty glasses, everyone fell away into different rooms and different activities for the remainder of the night. None of which were inviting to a precocious five-year-old.

1. The Dining Room Table

"Bullshit. He didn't have anything to do with it," Daddy grumbled, pushed back from the head of the table with his belt loosened, pensively working a toothpick.

Earlier that year, we'd watched the Watergate hearings gavel-to-gavel on TV, and the story remained at the center of the news. Agnew had resigned months prior, and President Nixon had delivered the infamous "I am not a crook" speech just weeks before, so of course it dominated conversation.

"He just got caught up in the cover-up," Daddy continued.

"Where there's smoke, there's fire, Dewey," Grandma said. "Agnew sure skedaddled in a hurry."

"That polecat," Daddy said. "Tax evasion, my ass. He was still on the take from his cronies in Baltimore."

"Nixon was smart to replace him with Ford. A Michigan man," Grandma said.

"And a Navy man," Daddy added. "He even played center for the Wolverines. Coulda gone pro."

"Well, if they impeach Nixon—" Mom said.

"Come on, Betty Lou," Daddy grumbled. "They can't impeach him."

"*If* they impeach him," she continued, "we'll have a Michigan man in the White House."

"Well as long as America stays discombobulated over this Watergate mess, those A-Rabs in OPEC will just keep raising oil prices," Grandma said. "Now who's gonna do something about that?"

"At this rate, gas will be fifty cents a gallon," Mom said.

2. The Kitchen Table

The kitchen table became the hub for cards and board games—Monopoly, Life, Trouble, chess, and checkers. Since we didn't have to get up for school the next day, this tournament could go on into the wee hours. Game time often turned to euchre, an obscure team card game that is wildly popular in the Midwest and relatively unknown everywhere else. Regardless of the game, playing always got competitive among the older kids. A five-year-old could learn a lot about trash-talking at the game table.

"Pass."

"It's your turn."

"Where's the dice?"

"If it was in your butt, you'd know."

"Oh yeah? Up your nose with a rubber hose."

"In your ear with a can of beer."

"Up your butt with a coconut."

"Off my case, toilet face."

"You think you're hot snot on a silver platter, but you're just cold boogers on a paper plate."

"Well, you look like you fell out of the ugly tree and hit every branch on the way down."

"I'm rubber, you are glue. It bounces off me and sticks to you."

"That was so funny I forgot to laugh."

"You're so ugly, your momma has to tie a pork chop around your neck just to get the dog to play with you."

"If my dog was as ugly as you, I'd shave his butt and teach him to walk backwards."

We roared laughing.

"Kids, keep it down now, this isn't a rumpus room," Mom yelled from the dining room.

3. The Living Room

The big event that night was *My Fair Lady* on TV for the first time, ten years after it was in theaters. When I asked Mom what it was about, she said Audrey Hepburn plays a poor wretched street girl who learns to be a proper lady. I liked her better in *Roman Holiday*, where she plays a proper lady who runs away to spend a day on the streets. Or *Wait Until Dark*, where she plays a blind girl who outsmarts the bad guys by breaking out all the light bulbs. I liked to think I would be that clever if I ever needed to be.

Breakfast at Tiffany's didn't make much sense to me at that age. I always lost interest before the sad parts. To a kid, Holly Golightly was a girl with her own apartment in a big city and a yellow cat without a name. How could she be anything but happy with so many friends, going to so many parties? I would imagine being Holly's best friend, sitting on the fire escape with her and stealing stuff from the dime store.

We sang the songs and danced around the living room— foxtrot to "Wouldn't It Be Loverly" and waltz to "I Could Have Danced All Night." We all grabbed a book and practiced walking with them on our heads, competing to see who could hold them on the longest.

"Hold your stomach in, Patricia Anne," Mom said. "From the side, you look like the letter *s*."

"The trick is," Grandma said, "imagine you have a balloon on a string. The string is tied to the top of your head, pulling you up. That's how you should always walk, girls. Head up, never slouch."

Without fail, every time we watched an Audrey Hepburn movie, they said the same things:

"She's so skinny. Look how tiny her waist is," Mom would say.

"I would kill to be that skinny," Mary would say.

"Me too," Karen would say.

11

---•---

They Do if They Have To

The next day, with no school and chores done, the big kids were angling to get to town to go to the movies. The Dawn Theater was showing *Badlands* with Sissy Spacek, about a fifteen-year-old girl who goes on a killing spree with her boyfriend.

"Mom, can I go?" I asked.

"Well…" Mom said.

"Please, Mom, no," Mary whispered, hoping I wouldn't hear. "We'll have to chase her, and we can't have fun if we have to babysit her."

"Babysit?!" I protested. "I'm *not* a baby!"

"You wouldn't like the movie anyway, Trisha," Karen said.

"How do *you* know?" I said, glaring.

"The car is already full," Dan said.

"Mom, please…" I begged, dragging *Mom* out into three syllables for emphasis.

"Maybe next time," she said.

I stomped up the stairs and flung myself on my bed. I kicked Catherine's bunk above me and wished terrible things on everyone involved. When they backed out of the driveway, I watched from my bedroom window, crying and cursing them all.

Mom called up for me to come downstairs.

"Do I have to?"

"Yes, you do. Right now."

I stomped back down the stairs. Furrowed brow, pursed lips, clenched fists.

"Go see your grandmother," Mom said.

Stomp, stomp, stomp.

"Get your boots on, you little pistol," Grandma said.

"Why? Where are we going?"

"You'll watch that tone with me, child," she said. "Your mom might put up with that sass, but I damned sure won't. Now get your boots and coat on. Now."

Attitude: adjusted.

"You too, Katie Catherine. Come on with us."

Once we were suited up and out the door, Catherine nudged me. "Cheer up, kiddo," she said and handed me a peppermint from her pocket.

Furrowed brow, pursed lips, clenched fists. Not gonna work this time.

"Whaddya say we get dirty and blow off some steam in the woods back there?" Grandma asked.

We walked for a while in silence.

"So what's eating you, Trishy-Anne-Trash-Can?" Grandma asked, a nickname I earned as a toddler because I wasn't a picky eater.

"I'm *sick* of being little!" I barked. "I'm always too little to do anything, and they get to do everything and leave me behind. It's not fair."

"They used to be little too, ya know. I know because I changed their diapers. Even I used to be little a long time ago. Can you believe that?"

My tiny five-year-old brain couldn't fathom that Grandma was ever a kid.

"Yeah. But I'll never catch up. I'll never be big enough to do anything fun."

"You're a kid. Your whole life is fun. Listen, someday they will be old fogies like your mom and dad, with jobs and bills and responsibilities, and they won't have time to do anything fun, and you'll still be young and free."

"I'll never be free. And nothing exciting happens here. Everything happens in cities like New York and Lost Angeles. That's where all the TV shows and movies happen."

"What about *The Waltons*?" Catherine said.

"That was in the olden times! Before cities were invented," I countered. "And nothing exciting happens on *The Waltons* either."

"What kind of excitement are you hoping for, child?" Grandma asked.

"I wanna explore jungles or dive for treasure in the ocean or catch bad guys like Kojak."

"Hmm. What about you, Katie Catherine?"

Catherine thought for a moment. "You know the guy on *Wild Kingdom*? Marvin Perkins?"

"Marlin Perkins."

"I want to be like his friend Jim, the one who gets to be around the animals."

"You already get to be around animals," she said, gesturing toward the barn.

"Just cows. I've been praying for a horse."

"A horse? That's a big responsibility. Do you think you can handle that?"

"Yes, ma'am. It's all I've ever wanted."

We got to the end of the lane and the edge of the woods. The creek was low enough we could step across without getting our feet wet.

"What's that saying?" Grandma pondered. "Into the forest we go to lose our minds but find our souls."

The northeast corner of the property is a mixed hardwood forest of maple, hickory, oak, and pine, just big enough for a kid to get lost in. The top canopy is high and thick, blocking sun and sheltering from rain. The understory is dense but clear enough to explore, crisscrossed by deer trails.

"Girls, do you hear that?" Grandma asked.

"Hear what?" Catherine answered.

"The birds, listen to all the birds."

"They're just birds, Grandma," I said.

"Just birds? *Just birds?* Do you know how many different kinds of birds are here? I can hear flickers and finches, blackbirds and warblers. Starlings. Do you know about starlings? Did you know they're not supposed to be here? They're English. From England!"

"Did they fly all the way here?" I asked.

"No, silly, birds can't fly that far," Katie Catherine said, tugging my braid.

"People brought them over by ship, around the turn of the century. Just a boxful of birds. And do you know why? Because Shakespeare mentioned them in one of his plays. Can you imagine? They let them loose in Central Park, in New York City."

"That's where Holly Golightly lives," I said.

"So every time you hear that '*ruh-ruh-WEE, ruh-ruh-WEE*,' that's a starling. And that bird—right here in your woods—is a direct descendant of those Shakespeare birds let loose in New York City a long time ago."

Catherine tried to whistle the call a few times. "*Ruh-ruh-WEE. Ruh-ruh-WEE.*"

"And the robin says, '*Cheer-up-cheerily, cheer-up-cheerily,*' and sometimes they whinny like a horse," she said, looking at Catherine. "And when there's a hawk around, they whistle. A really high-pitched whistle."

"Why?" I asked.

"Because a hawk will eat them and their babies," Catherine said.

"Nuh-uh," I said. "Birds don't eat other birds."

"They do if they have to," Grandma said.

"What's your favorite bird, Grandma?" Catherine asked, changing the subject.

"I love the chickadee. He's tiny and looks like he's wearing a fancy little tuxedo with a white bib and a black top hat. They're not afraid of people; they'll eat out of your hand if you hold still. They're little, but they're friends with a lot of other birds—bigger birds. And when they make an alarm call, everyone listens. Sometimes the little ones have big jobs," she said, nudging my shoulder.

"What's their song?" I asked.

"They have lots of calls. Their alarm sounds like 'CHICK-a-dee.' But their song, the way they talk to each other, is 'FEE-bee, FEE-bee.'" She whistled it a few times and waited for one to reply.

We strolled around the woods, picking up feathers, leaves, and pretty rocks. Grandma taught us the names of trees, which berries not to eat, and the difference between coniferous and deciduous trees. She stopped at an oak tree and pointed out some scratches on the bark. "See this, girls? This is where a buck has been rubbing his antlers."

"Why do they do that?" Catherine asked.

"Their antlers fall off every year in the spring. When the new ones grow back, they have a velvet cover on them, and it itches. They rub that velvet off, and it leaves their scent to mark their territory."

I rubbed the mark and smelled my fingers. Didn't smell like anything to me.

"And see here?" Grandma said. "See the deer trails? You can track them all through these woods and look for the antlers that fell off. I'll bet you find some. And other animal bones. Maybe a skull or jawbone. Because bones stay forever."

"We could collect them," Catherine said.

"Mom would hate that," I said, grinning.

"You know what else you can find here?" Grandma said. "Arrowheads. Indian arrowheads. Or a necklace made with animal bones and teeth. Maybe one of their bowls or tools."

"Nuh-uh!" I said.

"Of course! Don't you know Indians used to live here?"

"Right here?" I asked, incredulous.

"Right here," Grandma said. "All over Michigan. Up north where I live, in the Thumb. Even in Detroit. *Michigan* is an Indian word. It means 'big water.'"

"Grandma, we've been learning in school about the Indians who lived here," Catherine said. "They were called the Potawatomi. It means 'fire people.' Trisha, remember Baw Beese Lake, where we went swimming? And we got chiggers? That's named after Chief Baw Beese, who lived here."

"You hear that? The Potawatomi," Grandma said. "They might have made a fort right here, somewhere in these woods. They might have camped out and hunted deer right here in these woods. They might have grown corn in your field hundreds of years ago."

"Nuh-uh, Indians like in the cowboy movies?" I asked, still skeptical.

"Yep, right here," Catherine said.

"Look down. Right now, you might be standing where an Indian chief stood a thousand years ago or a hundred years ago," Grandma said, pointing at my feet.

"With feathers in his hair?" I asked, fingering my pigtails.

"With feathers in his hair. And maybe paint on his face. And maybe he rode a spotted horse with a ring around its eye."

I stood looking down at my feet, scraping the ground with my toe, as if I would conjure an Indian straight out of the pine straw.

"If you find an arrowhead, it might have been used to hunt animals, to hunt deer to feed their families, and to make clothes and blankets."

"Or buffalo," Catherine added. "Yeah, Mr. Lindstrom said there used to be buffalo here. And wolves and cougars and bears. Can you imagine a big black bear right here?"

"And that same arrowhead," Grandma continued dramatically, as you do with a child when you want their attention, "it might have been used to kill a bad guy. Because they had to reuse their arrowheads, you know. They made them by hand; they couldn't just go to the store and buy more. Maybe there was a fight or a battle right out in that field and"—she held up her long arms like she was shooting a bow and arrow—"and *whoosh, bam*—kills a bad guy. He dies somewhere in here, his body rots and leaves behind…an arrowhead for you to find, hundreds of years later."

"Like in the movies?" I asked, holding my arms like I was shooting a bow and arrow.

"Just like in the movies, but for real. Not acting. You know, all you see in those movies happened for real right here. In *your* woods. And you get to explore it every day."

"Like the movies…" I pondered.

We wandered around the woods, kicking through leaves, looking for treasures. Grandma quizzed us on trees and bird calls until we got them right.

"You're right, kiddo. You do have to wait 'til you're older to explore the world," Grandma said. "But until then, you have your own world here. Treasures to find, trees to climb. Look around. Maybe you can't dive in the ocean yet, but you have your own creek right here. In summer when the water is high, you'll have a place to cool off and look for fish and frogs, all to yourself. Do you think you'd have any of this in a city? You ask your mom sometime what it was like growing up in the city. All she and her brother had was a tiny yard, houses on each side, no room to run. Nothing but brick and pavement. Only sparrows. No water—none you'd dare play in."

"Yeah, Mom grew up in the city. Daddy too," Catherine said.

"You belong here. The both of you. The other kids are city kids, too far gone by the time you moved here. You can't grow roots on pavement. But you girls. You weren't born here, but you'll grow here. I can see it in your eyes. This is in your blood now. You have this dirt under your nails, this clean air in your lungs. You belonged to this land long before you stepped foot on it. This. This is the setting for your story."

Grandma whistled *CHICK-a-dee, CHICK-a-dee*, and Catherine whistled back *FEE-bee, FEE-bee*.

"Give it a try, Trisha," Katie Catherine said.

"I don't know how to whistle," I answered. "Or climb trees."

Grandma stopped in her tracks.

"Well?" I said, looking from Grandma to Catherine. "No one ever taught me."

"Well, we're not leaving these woods until you can," Grandma said.

Hours later, we returned to the house with feathers in our hair, berry stains on our cheeks, and pockets full of rocks. Catherine whistled *CHICK-a-dee*, and I whistled back *FEE-bee, FEE-bee*.

12

December 1973

The house was filled with Christmas carols and the aroma of pancakes when we got back after chores. Perry Como was jingle belling and harking the herald angels on the record player while Mom put a huge platter of pancakes on the table. They weren't fluffy like the picture on the box. They were pocked and spongy, but they were as big as a plate, and that's how Daddy liked them. Thank god there was always peanut butter and plenty of Aunt Jemima syrup on the table.

Mom was quiet and had a grin on her face like she knew a secret. "Go ahead, dear," she said, pressing Daddy's hand. "Tell them."

"Soon as you kids finish breakfast, I want you to get your coats and boots back on," Daddy said gruffly without looking up from his plate. "I have a job for you."

A job for you. When Daddy says he has "a job for you," your chest tightens. You don't dare roll your eyes or whine, but you know your day is ruined. Since we'd moved to the farm, "a job for you" had included everything from digging six hundred fence postholes to putting up six hundred bales of hay. Being little didn't get you out of jobs, you just did the part of the job you could handle. I couldn't lift an axe, but I could carry and stack wood.

We ate our pancakes in silence, looking at each other from face to face like we were in a poker game. Mom still had that grin on her face, but she was hard to read. Was it joy or sadism? She was the kind of pretty where, when she smiled, she could look either like a beauty queen or deranged.

With full bellies and long faces, we quietly donned coats, hats, scarves, mittens, and boots and waited outside. I shot questioning glances at the older ones but just got shrugs in response.

"C'mon," Daddy said, heading west down the road. "I'll be right back," he said as he ducked into the garage.

Once he was out of earshot, Karen said, "Ask him what we're doing."

"Why me?" I asked.

"Because *you're* his baby," she quipped. "He won't yell at you."

Daddy came out of the garage with a hacksaw and some rope. "Let's go," he said. The snow was deep, so we walked behind him in the tracks made by neighbors' trucks, like a line of cartoon ducks.

Coming from Detroit, we had seen plenty of snow, but never like this. City snow gets plowed and dirty almost as soon as it hits the ground. Country snow lies like a lazy blanket on the land, wind blowing it into billowy drifts across the roads and against the sides of red barns.

Mary fell back next to me, motioning toward Daddy, whispering, "Go ask him."

"No," I mouthed back.

She pinched my coat sleeve. "Go ask him."

"No!" I whispered.

"Brat." She romped back up to her position in line.

"You kids alright back there?" Daddy asked.

"Yes, Daddy," we said in unison.

Catherine hissed over her shoulder, "Don't be a baby."

Steeling myself, I bolted ahead through the snow and sidled up next to Daddy. I punched my small mitten into his big hand.

He squeezed my hand and smiled down at me. I threw a look over my shoulder and smiled. Dan shook his head and rolled his eyes.

"Daddy?"

"What, little girl?"

"Um, where are we going?"

"You'll see."

"Daddy?"

"What, little girl?"

"Are we almost there?"

"Almost there."

We turned at Lamb Road and then crossed the creek over the tractor path. About a quarter mile in, right in the middle of nothing but flat fields for miles around, stood a hill covered with evergreen trees. It looked like a mythical giant had pushed his head up out of the ground and grew trees for hair. It just didn't seem to belong there.

"OK, we're here," said Daddy. "Pick out a tree."

"A tree for what?" Dan asked.

"A Christmas tree."

In the city, we always had a fake tree. A gaudy shiny silver aluminum tree that came out of the box with its own stand. It was only three feet tall, so it sat on top of the TV. That wouldn't do now that we were a country family. Nothing less than Norman Rockwell would do.

We ran to the hill, losing ourselves in the trees. "This one!" one would yell. "No, *this* one!" We must have called out a dozen trees before we found one that we all liked and that—more importantly—Mom would like. I went for the pine trees with long shaggy needles and strong scents, but we ultimately went with a cone-shaped spruce. Daddy cut it down, and we used the rope to drag it home.

Later that day, after decorating the tree, we returned to what was henceforth known as Christmas Tree Hill for some of the greatest sledding in all of Hillsdale County. We brought our flimsy plastic Ronco sleds, and the Kjellberg kids brought a real toboggan, a hubcap, and a lawn mower hood with a braid of binder twine attached. We all took turns trying each of the sleds until we had adopted our favorites. Turns out my little butt fit best in the hubcap, and the Kjellberg boys preferred to toboggan with Mary and Karen. Go figure.

Christmas Day
1973

Betty owned the holidays.

Years before we left Detroit, a neighbor kid had told me the Easter Bunny wasn't real just weeks before Easter. My faith shaken, I informed my mom I would be staying up all night to see him with my own eyes, and if he didn't show, he wasn't real. Of course I fell asleep on the couch, but when I woke, not only were our baskets full of candy, but there was also a trail of large bunny prints in the snow leading up to the door. Straightened me right out, and I had no more doubts after that.

Years later, I learned that Mom had tied cardboard cutouts to her shoes to make the prints and restore my faith. She also had a talk with the neighbor kid's mom. We didn't see him again after that.

Yes, Betty owned the holidays. And no one—especially not some snot-nosed brat—was going to rob her of that. Even in the lean years, she never scrimped on holidays. Beg, borrow, or steal, we would have a birthday cake, an Easter basket, and presents under the tree.

———————•———————

On Christmas mornings, the rule was we had to sing "Happy Birthday" to Jesus before we were allowed to open presents. "You kids need to remember the reason for the season," she would scold. Usually the first up, I would dash down the stairs in my nightie, singing it so fast—happybirthdaytoyouhappybirthdaytoyou—I could get the whole song out before I hit the bottom step.

We started with our stockings, and it was my job as the youngest to pass them out. Mom (or Santa) would put an orange in the toe of our stockings, then some nuts and wrapped candies, then a few small gifts, and top it off with a candy cane. She always made a concerted effort to make sure we got the same or at least equivalent stockings. Our first Christmas at the farm, we all got little Bibles with our names embossed on the covers, and the girls got diaries with locks and tiny keys.

"Girls, those diaries are from your grandma," Mom said.

"What do I do with a diary?" I asked.

"You tell it your secrets."

"You record all the things you do."

"You keep track of your hopes and dreams."

"And then you lock it up so no one else can see it," Mom said.

Karen and Mary both trained their eyes on me.

"What?" I asked. "What did I do?"

"You better stay out of my diary, you little snoop," Mary said, clutching hers to her chest.

"Yeah, I'm keeping mine locked, so don't even try," Karen said.

"Don't say 'yeah,' dear," Mom said. "Patricia Anne, you better stay out of your sisters' things, OK? If I find out you've been snooping again…"

"Who, me?"

So no one can see it. Hmmph. Privacy was wishful thinking for anyone under that roof. That "baby of the family" chip on my shoulder drove me to sneak and snoop for any forbidden information. I would eavesdrop on teen phone conversations and pillow talk between parents. Leave me behind when you go to the game or a movie, and I'd be rifling through your stuff. What I couldn't have in fun and freedom, I would find in secrets under your mattress.

Later, we were all tearing open presents while Elvis sang about blue Christmases and white Christmases, silver bells and Parson Brown. Mom leaned by the picture window, watching us, sipping her tea and occasionally looking outside as snow fell against the house. With every excited "Mom, look what Santa brought me!" she would feign surprise and tell me I had better take care of it or Santa would take it away.

As the gift opening was winding down, she kept her eyes on the clock and the window. "Katie Catherine," she said. "Come here—there's something I want you to see."

Walking up the road toward the house was the neighbor girl Missy Kjellberg leading a skinny, scrawny, scruffy buckskin gelding. Before the rest of us even knew what was going on, Catherine was out the door in just her nightie and boots.

"Don't slam the door!" Mom yelled.

Slam.

I made it to the window just in time to see her run to him. He spooked and balked back a few steps. They exchanged puffs of frosty breath as she gently reached out to his muzzle, and he sniffed her tiny hand. For a moment, she was frozen, as if unable to comprehend that her prayers had been answered. He poked his big nose into her dark curly hair, and she threw her arms around his neck.

He would be named Dusty. He was what is called a junk horse. By chance, Mom had met a breeder at the fairgrounds who said his pedigreed full-bred grand champion Arabian with all kinds of trophies and titles and a huge stud fee had broken down a fence to get into a paddock with an unregistered mixed breed mare who was in heat. Dusty was too small to keep as a workhorse and not worth the price of the grain to feed him, so he was headed for auction, which likely meant slaughter. Mom gave the guy fifty bucks on the spot and made arrangements for him to drop the junk horse off at the Kjellberg's the week before Christmas.

Daddy had to force Catherine to come back in the house long enough to put some clothes on, then she was gone. She led Dusty around the yard, up and down the road, in and out of the barn. She made a stall for him on the upper side of the barn, away from the cows. We scavenged buckets and crates for his food and water, and "borrowed" a hammer and nails to build a stall door.

Until then, the big red barn had been a "have to" place. You have to get up early for chores, you have to shovel manure, you have to carry buckets. Dusty made it a "want to" place. A "love to" place for Catherine and me. His buckets of water were never heavy, and his shit didn't stink. He was the reason we learned to pee outside. We couldn't wait to get there every morning, and we hated leaving every night.

Dear Diary,

This is my first diary so I dont know what to write. chrismas was fun. catherine got a horse dusty. he is pretty.

i like my presents very much. thank you santa.

1. teddy bear name ted

2. breyer horse

3. play do

4. barel of monkeys

5. books

6. cloths and soks

Love

Trisha

Dear God,

Thank you for hearing my prayers. Thank you thank you thank YOU!

You are a great God.

Dusty is a beautiful horse and I love him. He is a buckskin with tan fur.

His mane and tail are black. He has a white star on his face.

I am excited to ride him.

God, I promise to take good care of him because he is your ~~creature~~ creation.

Amen
Katie Catherine

Job 39:19-25

14

Whoa, Boy

Everything she knew about how to break a horse, she learned from watching Westerns.

In the movies, there is always a lot of bucking and snorting and getting thrown in the dirt. Katie Catherine wanted to take it slow with Dusty, starting with empty feed sacks on his back, tied with baling twine. He didn't seem to care much about those. She didn't have a saddle yet, so she stole a couch cushion and tied it to his back. She worked up to a sack of grain on his back. He bucked a little, but mostly he just wanted to eat the grain.

When they were ready, Catherine stood on a tailgate and slowly lowered herself onto his back. He shook his head, let out a huff, shot straight up in the air like a cricket, landed on all fours, and then froze. Catherine held on and came back down, steady in her seat. She leaned down from his back and patted his neck, whispering to him until he relaxed. I don't know what she said, but when she finally nudged him with her heel, he twitched his ears and stepped forward. Within hours, Catherine had him walking and trotting. Within days, they were walking, trotting, cantering, galloping, stopping, and backing.

At every step and stage, I was there, perched on the top rail of the paddock fence and watching their every move. In that time, I saw my sister change. She walked differently. I think she even grew a couple inches. This timid, skinny waif transformed into a strong, confident girl. I'm no child psychologist, but I'm going on record as saying that learning to ride a horse is the very best experience a kid—especially a girl—could have. Remember what it felt like to learn to ride a bike? That sense of achievement? It's kinda like that, but the bike is a thousand-pound animal that can crush you. And not by accident—on purpose. Alternatively, that animal can learn to respond to your commands and do the most magical things. And do them not just for you, but *with* you. Together, as a team. It's a trust and mutual respect that you can't experience with an inanimate object or even another person.

When you're a kid and everyone is always telling you what to do, having that kind of relationship with a creature that could stomp you into the dust is a huge confidence boost. When you're a girl, you have so many occasions in your life when you're told what you can't do. When you learn early on what you *can* do, that lesson never leaves you.

———————•———————

After a few weeks, she let me ride on his back while she led him around. If he started to trot, I would squeal and grab his mane. After a few months of that, she had had enough.

"You're gonna learn how to ride for real," she said.

"What? I can't. I'm too little."

"You are not, you're five years old. Didn't you tell Grandma you were sick of not being allowed to do things? So quit being a baby."

She unhooked the lead, but Dusty just walked obediently at her side. "Now take up the reins and turn him," she said.

"I can't!"

"Yes, you can."

Like a dumbass, I squeezed with both legs, and Dusty bolted, running at full clip. I panicked and dropped the reins, clinging to his mane and screaming like a banshee. We made it to the corner of Rumsey Road, where he skillfully peeled me off on the stop sign. To this day, I can still hear the clang of the metal. When I came to, I was flat on my back in the ditch with Catherine standing over me.

"What the heck did you do?" she yelled. "You know better than that. Get up!"

She put out her hand to help me up like she always did. Once I got my breath, I started crying and rubbing all the sore spots, including a growing goose egg on my forehead. When we finally caught up with Dusty, one rein was snapped in half, so she tied it to the end of the other.

"Now get back up there."

"No! He hates me! He'll race off again!"

"Quit being a baby! This is the only way you're ever gonna learn how to ride. When you fall off, you get right back up there and try again. No little sister of mine is gonna be a quitter."

Still crying and smarting from the fall, I stepped to his side. "Come here, kiddo," she said and wiped my snot on her sleeve. She looked me in the eye. "You're not a quitter, are you?"

"No." *Quiver, quiver.*

"You're not a baby, are you?"

"No." *Sniffle, sniffle.*

She cupped her hands into a stirrup. Trusting, I put my boot in her hands and swung my leg over Dusty's back. She held the rein and walked by Dusty's side for a while, reminding me to keep my butt on his back, my legs relaxed, and my elbows bent. When she let go, I gave him a gentle nudge with my heel and got a good trot. When he lunged, I pulled the reins and checked him back to a trot. *Whoa, boy.*

Dusty was now the center of our universe. Catherine revolved around him, and I revolved around her.

15

Spring 1975

"Patricia Anne, stop scratching!" Mom yelled.

"But it itches!" I yelled back.

Catherine had caught chicken pox from a kid at school, and then she gave it to me. Now we were stuck at home, quarantined until we were no longer contagious. I was in the bumps and blisters stage, and she was in the blisters and scabs stage.

"You're gonna get scars if you keep scratching," Mom said. "Do you want me to get the oven mitts again?"

To keep me from scratching the blisters bloody, Mom had me cut my fingernails down to the quick and made me wear oven mitts. Once she discovered I was pulling them off every few minutes to scratch, she taped the wrists. They did help stop the scratching but quickly became a logistic problem. How could I hold pencils or crayons? Or pick up a cup of Vernors? And don't get me started on trying to go to the bathroom with them.

Catherine was better behaved, as usual. Instead of scratching, she methodically applied pink calamine lotion to her crusty spots. She was determined to get better so she could get back down to the barn with Dusty. Mom said we were too sick to help with chores, and Daddy said if we were too sick to do chores, we were too sick to be "down at the barn, scratching that damned horse's ass."

That didn't stop us from sneaking out of the house to see Dusty every chance we could. If Mom left to go to the store, we were at the barn. While she was distracted by Avon business, we put pillows under our blankets and sneaked out. One day, she was resting on the couch because she had a "splitting" headache. She put a cold washcloth over her eyes and told us to color quietly at the kitchen table. Knowing she would be down for at least an hour, Katie Catherine went to the barn, and I was her lookout. When I heard Mom start to stir, I whistled *FEE-bee, FEE-bee* out the kitchen window, and Catherine answered back *CHICK-a-dee, CHICK-a-dee*. She was back at the table in two shakes of a lamb's tail, and Mom was none the wiser.

After the big kids left for school, I would sneak upstairs and snoop through Mary and Karen's stuff, like their makeup and jewelry. They each had one of those little satiny jewelry boxes with the tiny ballerina inside. She would pop up on a little spring when you opened the lid and pirouette until the music stopped.

Mary and Karen hid their diaries and wore the keys around their necks. Once I found their hiding spots, it didn't take me long to figure out that all our diaries were the same brand and that my key would work to open theirs. You just had to jiggle it a little. Mary wrote mostly about boys and books; Karen kept track of her favorite songs and friends' secrets.

————————————•————————————

We got unlimited Popsicles and Vernors ginger ale, whiling away the days drawing horses and watching daytime television. In 1975, there were only four channels: ABC, CBS, NBC, and a public television station. Our favorites were *The Price Is Right* and *Wheel of Fortune*. We got pretty good at guessing the prices of blenders and dining sets and speed boats. We made up our own wheel of fortune puzzles to quiz each other. Mine were always candy bars (Reese's Peanut Butter Cups, Necco Wafers), and hers were always horse breeds (Thoroughbred, Arabian, quarter horse).

After game shows, Mom would take a break and watch the twelve o'clock news with us. I tried to make sense of the Vietnam War and the Weather Underground, and took special interest in Patricia Hearst's kidnapping because we shared the same name.

"Mom, why did she help rob the bank with the bad guys who kidnapped her?" I asked.

"She was brainwashed," Mom answered.

"What is brainwashed? They took her brain out and washed it?"

"No, it's just when people tell you the same thing over and over until you believe them."

Pause.

"That sounds like church," I said.
"Patricia Anne!"

———————•———————

For the whole week, Channel 11 was promoting their Saturday night movie, *The Ten Commandments* with Charlton Heston. They played the teaser at least once in every commercial break, using the climactic scene where Moses stands on the rock, parting the sea. After about the fortieth time hearing it, we could recite the lines along with the TV without even looking up from our books. Sometimes we would stand up and shout "Behold!" or "Let my people go!"

Before cable and VCRs, you could only see big movies like *The Wizard of Oz* or *Gone with the Wind* once a year when they were on TV, so they became an event. Families would watch together with root beer floats and big bowls of popcorn, kids sprawled across ugly shag carpet with sofa pillows and afghans.

No pause or rewind meant two things: absolutely no talking during the movie, and if you didn't want to miss anything, you went to the bathroom during commercial breaks. In a house with seven people, three-minute commercial breaks, and one bathroom—you do the math.

When it came time for the big *Ten Commandments* night, I didn't want to miss any of my favorite parts—water turning to blood, a snake eating another snake, the parting of the water— so I held my pee as long as I could. When I couldn't hold it anymore, I made a break for the bathroom, but someone was already in there.

"Hurry up, I gotta pee!" I yelped, hopping around and holding my crotch.

Dan finally emerged. "That's whatcha get for drinking a gallon of root beer, brat."

Dashing back to the living room, I dove headfirst into my spot on the floor just as Yul Brynner was breaking the good news to Moses, letting the Hebrews go.

"What did I miss?" I asked.

"The curse that killed all the firstborn," Katie Catherine said.

"I missed the green smoke of death?!" I cried.

"Yep."

Before I could even think about it, I belted out at full volume: "Dammit!"

Cue record scratch.

"Patricia Anne!" Mom yelled.

She grabbed my arm and yanked me out of the room. In TV shows, the mom would wash her kid's mouth out with soap and send them to bed. Instead, my mom just took me to the kitchen and gave me the what for. She reminded me that my birthday was coming up and I needed to be on my best behavior. She made me go to the living room and apologize to everyone. I stood there like a dope, red-faced, and stammered, "I'm s-s-sorry I cussed."

"Get out of the way, dummy, the movie's on," Dan said, pushing me out of the way.

Dear Diary,

Tonight we watched the 10 commandments on T.V. Karen thinks Charleton Heston is gorgeous but I think John Derek is way cuter. Almost as cute as "you know who."

At Track practice Coach made us run sprints. He thinks we have a chance at regionals if we all work really hard.

GO WILDCATS!

A weird thing happened after practice, Mr. Clark drove up and said he would drive us home. It was very nice of him because his kids don't even go to Pittsford. But then when Dan came out of the locker room, Mr. Clark drove off without us. ??? **BANANAS!**

I have $16 saved from babysitting. I charge 50c but Kelly said some people in town pay 75c an hour! I'm saving up for roller skates.

Signing off for now so I can get back to reading my book. It's about a girl named Audrey Rose. I don't know what it's about yet so I'll have to tell you later.

xoxo

Mary

16

Covet

Thou shalt not covet thy neighbor's house, thou shalt not covet thy neighbor's wife, nor his manservant, nor his maidservant, nor his ox, nor his ass, nor any thing that [is] thy neighbor's.

—EXODUS 20:17

"Patricia Anne, sit still," Mom said.

Sunday sermons are just hell on a kid; they're too long, the subject matter is boring, and the language is incomprehensible with all those *thees* and *thous*. Mom would try to placate me with gum or hard candy from the bottom of her giant purse, but I could not be bought off with a stale butterscotch or a Life Saver that tasted like perfume.

I couldn't draw Catherine into my shenanigans either because she was hanging on every word. If I tried to get her laughing, she would just pop me on the leg and shush me.

Luckily, my parents weren't overtly religious, just enough to leave a mark. I don't remember going to church in the city, but after we moved to the country, Mom made sure we went enough to make a good impression.

I always had questions after church.

Why did God tell Abraham to kill his kid? Was he *that* bad? If God asked you to kill me, would you do it? Did Jesus know how to swim? If Jesus is God's son, isn't God bigger than Jesus? So why pray to Jesus instead of God? Why didn't Jesus's friends stick up for him? I would have stuck up for him, and then he wouldn't have had to die. Why didn't God kill the soldiers with the green smoke? How can the devil be an angel? Why was it wrong for Eve to eat the apple when apples are good for you? Why didn't God want her to know anything? Didn't she go to school? When Adam and Eve had kids, who did their kids marry because they couldn't marry each other? When Noah's ark finally landed and the two elephants had babies, who did those babies have babies with? They couldn't have babies with each other because they'd be deformed.

You can't raise a kid on a farm and teach them animal husbandry and then be surprised when they don't buy the Bible stories.

———————•———————

We usually just went for the sermon because Bible school was too early. On one of those rare Sundays when we got there early enough, my Bible school lesson focused on the book of Exodus and the Ten Commandments. I hadn't read the book, but I was feeling pretty cocky about it because I had seen the movie. My hand shot up when the teacher asked for volunteers. She had ten of us stand in front of the class, each with a cardboard cutout of a Ten-Commandment tablet with a commandment written on it in big black marker.

My assigned commandment that morning was "Thou shalt not covet." One by one, the teacher went through the lineup and discussed each commandment. First, she would ask the poor soul holding the card to read it and tell the class why God would give us this commandment. Don't kill, don't steal, don't worship other gods, go to church, be nice to your parents. All pretty easy. Except the one about adultery—she skipped over it quickly and conveniently by telling us that "adultery can only be committed by adults, so you don't have to worry about it for now."

Then she got to me.

"Thou shalt not covet," I said aloud.

"And why would God tell us not to covet?" the teacher asked.

Crickets.

"You don't know why God would not want us to covet?" she asked.

"I don't know what covet is, ma'am," I said. "That wasn't in the movie."

A few giggles and whispers from the more veteran Bible schoolers. Some of them shot up their hands to answer the question for me.

"Hush now, children," she clucked. "What is your name, dear?"

"Trisha."

"Well, Trisha. To covet is to look upon your neighbor's things and want them. To desire them. To wish that you yourself could own them. Do you ever want your neighbor's things?"

"My neighbors' things? Do you mean their cows and tractors and stuff?"

More giggles.

"No, not literally your neighbors. Your peers, your friends. Do you ever find yourself wishing you had what they have, wanting to own their possessions?"

"But isn't that the same as stealing?" I retorted, gesturing toward kid number four with the no-stealing commandment.

"Even if you don't take it, it's wrong to covet your neighbor's things, dear."

"If I don't take it, how would anyone know I coveted it?"

"God knows your every thought." She turned to the class. "Children, what about the things you see on television? Or in the store? Do you covet those toys and those games you see on television?"

"Well, yeah. Everybody does," I said. "That's what we ask Santa to bring us for Christmas."

Before she could respond, the bell rang, signaling the end of class and our call to get upstairs for the sermon. She told us to take our commandments with us, and we filed out of the room. Upstairs, the choir was singing while we took our seats in the pews.

O precious is the flow
That makes me white as snow
What can wash away my sin
Nothing but the blood of Jesus

Halfway through the sermon, the pastor told the congregation that Miss Whatsername's class had something to share with them from today's lesson. She took the stage and instructed the commandment kids to please come forward. Mom beamed and scooted me off to the stage. After arranging us in order of our commandments, the teacher called on each of us to read our commandment and tell what we had learned in class. Some of the kids got a little stage fright. Even one of the kids with an easy one couldn't seem to get the words out, so the teacher helped him. I could see the trepidation on her face when she got to me, but I was feeling confident. This would be my big moment.

"Thou shalt not covet," I proclaimed.

I scanned the crowd, looking for my mom's face. Her eyes were expectant, her brows set up high. All my siblings sat forward to see me. Daddy gave me a big smile. I could even see his silver crown shining in his mouth. I would make them all so proud. Maybe I would get a standing ovation. Maybe they would carry me out on their shoulders like on TV.

"And why doesn't God want us to covet?" the teacher asked, leaning toward me with the microphone.

"God doesn't want you to want your neighbor's stuff, but not cows and tractors. Just toys. And don't wish that you had your friends' toys or what you see on TV. So don't ask Santa for toys because that will make Moses mad. But it's OK to ask for a cow."

A few snickers from the congregation and a nervous laugh from the pastor. No cheers or standing ovation.

"Uh, ha ha...well, I...uh..." the teacher trailed off as the pastor took the mic back.

"That's just fine," he said. "Thanks, kids. You can go back to your seats now."

———•———

"Mom, what do *you* say covet means?" I asked from the back seat on the way home.

"Well, didn't you learn that in Bible school?"

"Yeah, but it didn't make any sense how Miss Whatshername said it."

"Don't say 'yeah,' dear."

"Yes, ma'am."

She looked at my dad with an exasperated face, and he just shook his head. "Don't look at me, she's *your* child."

"When you covet something," Mom said, "you look at it and want it and want to make it your own. You want to own it."

Pause.

"When you and Daddy bought the car, you looked at a bunch of them until you found the one you wanted. And then you bought it. So you own it, right?"

"That's different, darlin'. We needed a car."

"So it's OK to covet if you need it?"

Mom sighed. "No. It's not coveting if you need it."

"But you already had a car."

"But we needed a new one. A bigger one."

Pause.

"So it's not OK to want stuff?"

"It's not OK to want other people's things."

"What if I want something *like* another person's things? But I want one of my own."

"That's jealousy," Karen said.

Dan piped in. "Besides, you have enough toys and junk. You get everything you want, brat."

"Daniel," Mom scolded.

Pause.

"What if I want something, but I can work for it and work until I can get it? Like Daddy does."

"That's what you're supposed to do, darlin.'"

Pause.

"But how do I know what I'm supposed to be working for if I can't covet it first?"

She let out a big sigh and looked at Daddy again.

He shook his head and chuckled. "She sure is your child, Betty Lou."

———————•———————

If you look just like a parent, people say you are their "spittin' image."

If you don't, people joke that you're the milkman's kid.

Remember how kids would fantasize they were cradle swapped in the hospital? That there was a terrible mix-up and their real parents were wealthy and doting, searching for their biological child all this time? And someday their real parents would find them and take them away to their real family, their real home?

Not me. I didn't look anything like my mom but never once doubted that I was Betty Lou's child. Like it or not, I could feel at a cellular level how I was connected to her—a part of her, as if I fell from her body like a bird's feather lost in flight.

Dear Diary,

Stuff I Covet

1. Loris swimming pool

2. Meullers trampoline

3. Becky Lynns Big Wheel

4. Marys Etch sketch

5. budwisers Clydesdales

6. Winnie Poohs treehouse with a frigerator

Stuff to ask Santa for Christmas

1. Mickey Mouse watch

2. stuff for Dusty

3. glow in dark Godzilla

4. Sleeping Bag

5. Bugs Bunny

6. snow Boots

Trisha

17

April 1975

"Mrs. White, we need to talk about Trisha."

It was the Friday before spring break. It had to be Friday because Mrs. Thacker was wearing the periwinkle-blue polyester pantsuit that matched her hair. She wore it every Friday, so I believed it was her favorite suit. And because it meant Fridays, it became my favorite suit too.

April meant two things: spring break and my birthday.

I can't overstate the importance of birthdays to a youngest. Turning five was special because it meant I was no longer a baby or a toddler. Turning six was special because it meant I wasn't a five-year-old anymore. And turning seven, well, now we're smack-dab in the business of being a kid. Needless to say, I had better things on my mind than minding my manners.

When I got home from school, I dropped my books on the stairs and headed right back out the door.

"Trisha darlin'?" Mom called from the kitchen in a sing-songy tone.

This could only mean one thing: she had something for me to do. Some god-awful chore or ridiculous, tedious, soul-crushing task that should never be asked of a child. Especially not on a glorious Friday afternoon in spring. I imagined her spending all day dreaming up shitty tasks, just waiting for us to get home from school so she could spring them on us and ruin our lives.

- "Get the stepladder and climb up to reach my good bowl in the top cabinet so I can make my potato salad. I can't reach it because my bursitis."

- "Take a Q-tip and that can of Pledge and clean the grooves in the woodwork on the front of the stereo. I can't bend down like that because my bad knee."

- "Take this box down to the basement and bring up a dozen canning jars. I can't stand those cobwebs."

- "Get the mayonnaise"—pronounced *may-nays*—"and a paper towel and polish the leaves on all the houseplants."

So I pretended I didn't hear her. If I could get to the barn without her seeing me from the kitchen window, I'd be home free. But I was too slow; she was on me faster than a sneeze through a screen door.

"Patricia Anne!"

"What?" I snapped.

"Don't you 'what' me, young lady. When I call you, you answer 'Yes, ma'am.'"

"Yes, ma'am."

"I got a call from Mrs. Thacker today."

"What? Why? I didn't do anything wrong."

"She said you've been getting in trouble and bothering the other kids."

"Nuh-uh. I was trying to help. I do my assignments, then help Becky Lynn with hers."

"There's more to school than doing your assignments. You have to behave yourself and mind your teacher. Follow the rules.

Do what she says, and if she says to shut your mouth and keep your butt in that chair, you do it."

"I try to behave."

"You'll have to try harder. If I get one more call from the school, you'll be grounded."

I held my head down, lip quivering, trying not to cry. "You won't tell Daddy, will you? Please don't tell Daddy."

"We'll see. I have something for you to do," she said, with one hand on her hip, squinting in the sun. Maternal extortion; the most efficient parenting tool at her disposal.

Over her shoulder, I noticed Karen and Mary peeking out the window. They jumped back when they saw me look. Something was up. Not only was it a chore, but she was going to somehow use it to humiliate me in front of my siblings.

"What is it?" I said, head cocked, brow furrowed, lips pursed, and arms crossed.

"I got another call. From the neighbors."

Neighbors? What? She's making me do chores for the neighbors now?

"But...what neighbors?"

"The Ramseys. They're going on vacation next week."

A week? What is she gonna make me do? Mow their lawn? Get their mail? Clean the poop out of their dog pens?

"All week? But it's spring break!"

"Oh, I'm sorry, do you already have plans?" she said sarcastically.

"Well...kinda."

"OK, I'll call them back and tell them you can't do it. They're going to Florida and need someone to take care of their pony, Shasta."

"Pony?"

Cue angelic choir sounds.

"Yes, the little brown one who lives in the field behind their house."

"A pony?!"

"Do you think you can do that?"

Yes, yes, yes!

"Yeah! What do I have to do?"

"Don't say 'yeah,' dear. After supper, you and Catherine will go down to their house and get her."

"Get her…tonight?!"

"Yes, tonight. After supper."

"I can bring her here? Can I keep her in the barn?"

"Of course in the barn, silly. Where did you think you would keep her, in your room?"

I stood with my hands on my head, mouth agape, my head spinning with possibilities. A pony. A real pony. Here. In our barn.

"Close your mouth, darlin," Mom said, "before you catch some flies."

"Her name is Shasta?" I asked. "Like the pop?"

"Yes, now you know you have to take care of her, right? You're responsible for feeding her and keeping her stall clean. Can you do that?"

"Yes! God, Mom. I can—"

"Patricia Anne! Don't take the Lord's name in vain. Don't say 'God' unless you mean it. He has more important things to worry about."

"Yes, ma'am," I said, dashing off. There was so much to do.

"And Patricia Anne…"

"Yes, ma'am?" I answered over my shoulder, barely pausing.

"If I get one more call from the school about your behavior, I *will* tell your father."

In the dining room, Karen and Mary were sitting at the table, smiling knowingly at me. Under any other circumstance,

I hated when they knew something before I did, but this time I didn't care.

"Did you hear?" I asked, panting. "Did you hear I'm taking care of the Ramseys' pony?"

"Yes. Brat," Karen said.

"You know you have to feed her, carry her water, clean her poop, and everything, right? We're not gonna do it for you," Mary said.

"I know," I said, perma-grinning. "I can do it. I took care of the calves last year, didn't I? By myself."

Catherine. Where was Katie Catherine? I had to tell Katie Catherine! I ran through the house to find her, but she was already at the barn.

"Don't run in the house!"

I dashed out the door.

"Don't slam the door!"

Slam.

When I got to the barn, Catherine was fixing the gate on the stall next to Dusty's.

"Hey kiddo."

"Did you hear? Did you?" I asked, panting.

"Yep. Mom asked me if I thought you could do it, and I said, 'Yeah, she can do it.'"

"You did?"

"Can you do it? Can you take care of her?"

"Heck yeah! I'm not a baby. I took care of the calves, didn't I?"

"Yeah, but this is different. I mean, I'll be here to help you, but you gotta do the work yourself."

"I know. I can do it."

We spent the next few hours getting the new stall ready. We checked every inch of every board for any nails sticking out and pounded them down. We pulled up splinters.

Checked the hinges and hook. I scraped the floor down to the dirt, and Catherine put down fresh straw. We hung a five-gallon bucket of water from a hook in one corner, a grain bucket in the other.

———————•———————

At supper, Mom said we couldn't leave until we finished everything on our plates. I was squirming and picking at the soggy veggies on my plate, my mind and mouth racing.

"Do you think she likes to trot?

"Will Dusty like her?

"Can I take her over to show Becky Lynn?

"How fast do you think she can run?

"Mom, can I have some ribbon to braid into her mane?

"Do you think she'll like grain?"

"Alright, alright. Just go," Mom said. "If you're not going to eat anything anyway."

We were in our boots and out the door before Daddy could say, "Betty Lou, look at all that food they're wasting."

"Don't slam the door!"

Slam.

When we got to the Ramsey house, we were met by a symphony of barking beagles in the driveway, and the oldest boy, Will Jr., answered the door.

"Yeah?"

"Uh, we're here to get the…your…uh…pony?"

"Have a seat. I'm almost done with supper," he said.

We looked at each other, but not knowing where to sit, we just stood by the door.

Will Sr. was the county sheriff, sitting at the table eating supper in his gray uniform, gun belt still on. He looked over his shoulder and caught me looking at his holster, and I looked away quickly. "Hi, girls. How ya doin'?"

"Hello, Sheriff," we said in unison.

"How's your mom and dad?" asked Mrs. Ramsey.

"Good."

"D'jer dad ever get that tractor runnin'?" Sheriff Ramsey asked.

"Yes, sir."

The three younger Ramseys, ranging in age from little to tween, strained to stare at us from the table. None of them were in our grades, but we all rode the same bus, so we knew each other. They were the kind of kids who only hung out with their siblings at recess, so I was naturally leery of them. We nodded acknowledgment to each other, a child's greeting. They went back to eating, keeping one eye on us.

Catherine and I stared at our shoes.

"You girls want some Kool-Aid?" Mrs. Ramsey called from the kitchen.

"No thank you, ma'am."

Now waiting through a second meal to get to that pony, I rocked from one foot to the other, impatient. Finally, Will Jr. came out of the kitchen, wiping his mouth on his sleeve. He pulled his boots on and went for the door without a word. We followed.

"Don't slam the door!" from the kitchen.

Slam.

He led us to a gate behind the shed that was behind the house. Weeds had grown over the latch. A small group of goats came trotting up, bleating for attention. I could see Shasta up the hill, pushing her head through the fence to graze. When she saw us at the gate, she let out a small whinny and started walking toward us.

"You brought a halter, right?" Will Jr. asked.

"Doesn't she have one?" I asked.

"Naw, she don't. Heck, nobody's done anything with her since I was a kid."

"Do you have a piece of rope? Or binder twine?" Catherine asked.

"Yeah, I'll get some," Will Jr. said, annoyed.

Catherine unwrapped a peppermint. "Here, give this to her."

I stepped through the fence as she approached, her ears forward and her eyes bright. She put her velvety muzzle in my hand. This was the first time I had seen her up close. She wasn't brown, she was just dirty. Filthy. Her coat was shaggy, and her mane and tail were full of burrs. Her ears were full of nettles. Mud and manure caked on her knees, and her hooves were overgrown and curled upward.

She was the most beautiful thing I had ever seen.

Catherine made a makeshift halter out of the bailing twine. I led Shasta out the gate while Will Jr. held back the goats.

"What does she like to eat?" I asked.

"I dunno, whatever she can get," Will Jr. responded. "She's eaten everything in that field."

"Does she like apples?" I asked.

"I guess."

As we walked past the house, Sheriff Ramsey stepped out on the porch. I could see his star and name tag, and it reminded me of Officer Reed from *Adam-12*. He took the toothpick from his mouth and said, "You enjoy her, girls, OK?"

"Thank you," we said in unison.

"I'll take good care of her while you're in Florida," I said, never taking my eyes off her.

"Oh, OK. Right. Tell your folks I said hello then."

"OK, Sheriff."

When we got home, I walked her around the yard for a while, talking to her and letting her munch on the grass. Dan was sitting on the front steps, tossing a baseball into his glove.

"What the heck is that thing?" he asked.

"It's a pony, what does it look like?" I said.

"It looks like the Creature from the Black Lagoon."

"Shut up! She does not," I snapped. "She just needs to be brushed."

"Brushed? Hmmph. More like shot. Put it out of its misery."

When I put her in her stall, she went right for the water bucket and drained it to the bottom. Catherine and I looked at each other as if she had done a trick.

"You go get her another bucket of water, and I'll get the grain."

She downed two more buckets while Dusty stood staring down at his new stablemate. He tried to initiate the perfunctory introductory muzzle sniffing, but Shasta was busy eating the straw off the floor of her stall. She had never eaten from a bucket, so she knocked it off the hook and spilled the grain on the floor. I scooped it up and fed it to her from my hands, her soft pink tongue working to catch every grain from my palm and between my fingers.

Catherine and I stayed at the barn until Mom yelled from the kitchen window for us to come in. And then we lingered a while longer until Daddy yelled out the door for us to "get your asses in the house right this goddamned minute, and don't make me tell you again or you're gonna be sorry."

Dear Diary,

This is the best day of my life. I get to take care of a pony her name is Shasta like the Pop. She is so pretty. She loves to eat and drink her water.

Dan says she is ugly but I say She is the best pony in the world.

She is nice and does not bite.

Love

Trisha

18

A Promise and a Hug

When I got to the barn the next morning, Shasta had eaten all her hay, all her grain, and all the straw off the floor, drained her water bucket, and knocked it off the hook. We were amazed at her appetite, and I was proud of her for being a good eater.

After chores, I couldn't wait to clean her up and see what was under that layer of mud and manure. I started with a currycomb but couldn't penetrate the shell of caked-on mud. She was going to need a full bath. Three buckets of sudsy water later, a pony began to emerge. I stole a big bottle of pink creme rinse from the house and saturated her mane and tail to get the burrs out. I stole Mom's fancy Fiskars sewing scissors to cut what didn't comb out and trim her whiskers and the tufts of hair from her ears. I stole towels to rub her dry while she stood still and patient, never fussing.

Under all that dirt, her real color wasn't a color at all but a dizzying pattern of silver gray with dark-gray spots on her back and rump. Her legs and belly were dark brown, as if she had been dipped in a vat of chocolate up to her chest. She reminded me of a fudge Pop-Tart, brown on the bottom with white icing and sprinkles on top. Her mane and tail were an unruly salt-and-pepper mix. No matter how much creme rinse and combing, her forelock always poofed up a bit. Her brown face was topped with a white star between her eyes and finished with a soft gray muzzle. She had a white ring around one eye.

Catherine borrowed a file from Daddy's garage to file her hooves down. I held her by her twine halter while Catherine picked up each hoof, pinned it between her skinny knees, and rubbed the file downward, just like we had seen blacksmiths do in all the Western movies.

When she was all squeaky clean, I walked her to the garage to show her off.

"Well how 'bout that?" Daddy said. "That's a real pretty pony, little girl. You did a good job."

"Thanks, Daddy. Isn't she pretty?"

Dan rolled out from under the truck he was working on.

"She still looks like a mule."

"Shut up! She does not."

"Hmmph," he clucked and rolled back under the truck.

Catherine and I put together a bridle, tying the headpiece up because it was too big for her. She hadn't been ridden in years, but you wouldn't have known it. She took the bit easily and didn't buck at all. She was still plow reined, so I had to turn her like a bicycle.

I was up early every morning to spend time with her before chores, and we were out riding right after. Mom sent the older girls to the barn with sack lunches so Catherine and I wouldn't have to come back to the house. Every night, we stayed at the barn until Mom yelled threats from the kitchen window.

———————•———————

Friday morning, I rushed to the house after chores and knocked on Mom and Daddy's bedroom door. "Mommy?"

"What?"

"Can I come in?"

"Wha-at?"

I went in and knelt by her side of the bed, where I could whisper without waking Daddy. "Do you think the Ramseys would want me to keep her through the weekend?"

"Phew, you stink. What, were you rolling in manure?"

"No, I must have got some on my pants."

"Well don't get it on my rug!"

"Sorry," I whispered. "Do you think they would mind?"

"Who?"

"Ramseys."

"Mind what?"

"If I watch her through the weekend. Shasta. In case they need time to unpack and stuff."

She smiled and took my hand. "You really like her, don't you?"

"Yeah, I do."

"Don't say 'yeah,' darlin'. Come here and let me fix your pigtails."

She sat on the edge of her bed and rebraided my hair. I wore my hair in pigtails every day from age five. When *Little House on the Prairie* came out, people started calling me Half-Pint.

"I'll tell you what. If you promise to wash this dirty hair tonight with no arguments, I'll call them and ask if she can stay for the weekend."

Leaving her with a promise and a hug, I dashed off back to the barn.

"Stop running in the house, and don't slam the door!"

Slam.

With that reprieve, I spent the weekend pretending she was an Appaloosa and I was a Potawatomi brave running with Chief

Baw Beese, imagining that he must have ridden in our woods sometime in the past.

And then it was Sunday night. Birthday eve. Any other year, I would be positively unbearable by the time my birthday rolled around. I would count down the days for at least a month, announcing to everyone how many days until my birthday and how old I was going to be. For a whole year, I had been so excited about turning seven. And then I was pony-sitting and totally forgot about my birthday. And now the latter was almost here, and the former was almost over. My birthday was no longer a special day but more like D-Day.

At supper, I was quiet and barely touched my food.

"Are you excited about your birthday tomorrow, Trisha darlin'?" Mom asked.

"Yeah, I guess."

"Don't say 'yeah.'"

"Yes, ma'am."

"They'll sing 'Happy Birthday' to you at lunch, right?" she asked.

"I guess."

"Well, we'll sing 'Happy Birthday,' too, when we have your cake and ice cream tomorrow night."

Tomorrow night. Who cares about cake and ice cream? All I could think about was that Shasta was going back tomorrow night. I felt my bottom lip quivering and my eyes welling with tears. A big cry was coming, and I couldn't stop it from happening. The only thing worse than crying in front of siblings is crying in front of siblings at the supper table, so I hightailed it upstairs to cry into my pillow. After a few minutes, Katie Catherine came up and sat next to me.

"Hey kiddo," she said, putting her hand on my back. "You gonna be OK?"

"I'm gonna miss her"—*sniffle*—"so much."

"I know. But you can go visit her. Anytime you want. I'll go with you. We can take apples and stuff to her. And peppermints. You know how she loves peppermints."

"Yeah"—*sniff, sniff*—"but it won't be the same."

She put her arm around me. "I know. I'll tell you what. I'll let you help me more with Dusty, OK?"

"Like what?" I asked, wiping snot on my sleeve.

"Like you can brush him more. And I'll let you braid his tail."

"But…she…she'll be all alone in that field."

"She'll be alright," Catherine said. "She lived out there for years, and she was OK."

"She was *not* OK!" I cried. "She was dirty, and she didn't have any grain or a stall to sleep in at night. And nobody loved her!"

I cried myself to sleep that night, right there in my dirty barn clothes.

Dear Diary,

I am very sad. Shasta has to go home tomorrow. I don't want her to go. She is the most best pony. She will be alone in the dark. No one loves her. But I love her more than anything or anyone.

I wish tomorrow would never come.

Trisha

19

Birthday 1975

In the morning, I was the last to come down the stairs.

While I was sobbing over the sink in the bathroom, Catherine knocked on the door. "C'mon, kiddo. We got chores to do."

"Can you...can you just...feed her for me?" I whimpered.

"What? Why?"

"I don't wanna..."

"Trisha!" Catherine said. "She's *your* responsibility, ya know?"

"I don't wanna...I can't...say g-g-good b-b-bye to her."

When I finally came out of the bathroom, my face red from crying, Mom and Catherine were waiting outside the door, arms crossed.

"You're not going to do your chores this morning?" Mom asked.

I shook my head, eyes welling, lip quivering.

She looked at Catherine and tossed her nose toward the door, motioning for her to leave. Catherine gave me a look and stomped off.

"Don't slam the door!"

Slam.

"C'mon and keep me company in the kitchen," Mom said.

I stood at the kitchen window, staring down at the barn. Dan was carrying the hose to the water trough. Karen carried buckets, and Mary threw a bale of hay down from the loft. From the back door of the barn, I saw Catherine lead Shasta out and toward the house.

"Mom! What is she doing? Why is she being so mean?"

I ran out, planning what I was going to say to her. *How dare you? What did I do to deserve this?* The big kids had stopped what they were doing and watched us from the barnyard. *Good,* I thought. *I want them to see this because I'm gonna let her have it. Just because I'm the baby doesn't mean you can be so mean.*

"*What* are you doing?" I yelled. "I *told* you I didn't want to—"

As I got closer, I noticed that Shasta was wearing a brand-new bright-red halter. My favorite color. There was a big white bow on the side, with a big tag that said "Happy birthday, Trisha."

"But...she...I..."

Catherine handed the lead line to me.

"Happy birthday, kiddo."

Dear Diary,

I am the happiest person in the world! I got my own
PONY!

She is my pony now and I will take the best care of her.
Mom said I can change her name so her new name is
Holly. She is my best friend.

It is my birthday today. And so it is Holly's birthday too. I
wonder how old she is.

I also got a snoopy watch

Daddy gave me a pocket knife for my birthday

Love

Trisha and Holly

20

Always Get Back On

I pledge my head to clearer thinking,
my heart to greater loyalty,
my hands to larger service,
and my health to better living,
for my club, my community, my country,
and my world.

—4-H PLEDGE

When I tell you I was an equestrian, don't believe me. I'm lying. I was just a horse girl.

Equestrians have purebred, papered, pedigreed horses registered by the official breed associations like the American Quarter Horse Association (AQHA). They have cheeky registered names—a combination of the sire's and the dam's so you know their lineage just by their name. So if Chance's Moonlight Whisper has a foal with Gambler's Midnight Runner, the foal's name might be Runner's Last Chance. Get it? Equestrians take years of riding instructions in indoor arenas while their horses are sent to professional trainers. They wear tight breeches and black velvet hunt caps with an upside-down bow on the back. Their tack rooms are climate controlled and reek of fine leather and silver polish. Their horses are kept in stables, not barns, put up at night with fresh sawdust under their always shod hooves and a fitted flannel blanket on their freshly groomed backs.

Horse girls have what are called "grade horses." Unregistered, no papers. Mixed breed or of questionable heritage. Mutts. Nags. Dog food. Elmer's glue on the hoof. They have simple two-syllable names like Dusty or Holly. Patches or Princess. Horse girls don't have trainers or riding instructors—they learn by falling off and getting back on. They wear jeans and dusty boots. Their tack is cheap, mismatched, and likely held together in a couple places with binder twine. It hangs on a nail outside a stall in a barn shared with livestock like cows and pigs.

————————•————————

Once Mom had two horse girls, she got us into a 4-H club, which, if you don't know, is like Girl Scouts for horse girls. We went to monthly meetings and learned basic horsemanship, grooming, health, and nutrition. We memorized the parts of a horse (Where's the forelock? Fetlock?) and learned to identify all the different breeds (What's the difference between an American saddlebred and a Tennessee walking horse?). We went on field trips to fancy horse shows and tours of grand stables. I would fall behind the group so I could sneak around and look at their stuff. I loved to run my fingers through the grain bin, a sticky-sweet mix of oats and corn that we could never afford. No one noticed when I filled my pockets to take home to Holly.

Ever the salesman, Mom would send us to 4-H meetings with baggies full of Avon samples. "Tell them how the Skin So Soft keeps the bugs away and how the One Step creme rinse gets burrs and knots out of tails," she would say. When we left the meetings, she had left catalogs under the windshield wipers of all the cars.

Catherine and I hung on every word, watched closely, and took copious notes and sketches. Some of the nicer 4-H leaders lent us books and gave us their old copies of *Horse & Rider* magazine. We argued over which Kentucky Derby winner was better, Man o' War or Secretariat. We ogled pictures of grand champions like they were centerfolds, taping clippings on the wall next to our bunk beds and sharing plans in whispers while we fell asleep.

"Katie?" I whispered.

No response.

"Katie Catherine?"

Still no response.

"Catherine?"

She always said her prayers after we got in bed and, as a rule, would not stop her prayers to answer my dumb questions. I should have learned this by the hundredth time, but it still always took at least three tries before I realized she was praying and not just ignoring me. For a kid, she had a lot to talk about with God. Sometimes I would forget my question while I was waiting for her to finish.

"What?" she finally said.

"Are we gonna practice again tomorrow?"

"Of course, dummy."

"What are we gonna practice?"

"Dusty needs more work on backing up."

"What about me and Holly?"

"You need to work on your seat so you stop bouncing when you trot."

"Yeah," I agreed.

"And keep your toes in."

"Yeah."

"You don't want the judges to mark you down for that, do you?"

"Judges?"

"Yeah, judges. You're gonna show at the fair with me this year, aren't you?"

"Show?"

"Yeah, the horse show. At the fair."

"But I'm too little."

"Pee Wee classes, dummy. For five- to ten-year-olds."

"But I…"

"But what? You've had Holly for months now, you've been working hard, you're getting better."

"Nuh-uh," I said, pushing my foot under her bunk. "Really? You think so?"

"Quit kicking…and yes, I think you're getting better."

"You think Mom will let us? How much does it cost?" I asked.

"I already asked her. She said maybe, as long as we both get good grades and do our chores and don't get grounded, she'll think about it."

"Grounded? I haven't been grounded since I said *dammit*."

"Well don't say it again!"

"What? No one can hear me. I'm whispering."

"Jesus can hear you."

"Sorry."

"Don't say sorry to me."

"Sorry, Jesus. Sorry, Santa."

———————•———————

Summer on a farm—even a fake farm—is anything but a vacation. In between baling hay, mending fences, and picking rocks, Catherine and I practiced and drilled. Without an arena, we made do with a low patch of the hayfield. Right by that stop sign, which still stands to this day as a reminder to always get back on.

"Keep your head up," Catherine would scold.
"Stop looking at her withers!
"Get those heels down, toes in!
"Shoulders back, elbows in!
"Keep your seat!
"Why are you bouncing all over?"

Proper riding form is unnatural, unintuitive, and uncomfortable. But it's proper, so you practice and practice until it feels natural. Keep your body in perfect vertical alignment: imagine a straight line drawn from your ears to your shoulders, shoulders to hips, hips to heels. Now drop your heels below your toes and point your toes straight forward so your feet are parallel with the horse. Go ahead and try—I'll wait. Suffice it to say, your ankles aren't meant to bend that way.

Now all you have to do is maintain that position no matter what gait your horse is in—walk, trot, or canter. Oh, and you have to maintain contact with the horse's back. That's called "keeping your seat." And to do that, you have to convert your entire torso into a spring, a shock absorber, and an accordion.

"Pretend your crotch is glued to her back!" Catherine would yell, and I would giggle because she said *crotch*.

We took turns blindfolding each other and turning our horses on a lunge line.

Breathe deep in your belly, let it out slowly.

Keep your balance.

Maintain your position.

Elbows in.

You're leaning forward.

You're leaning back.

Where are your reins?

Where are your hands?

It was a lot to remember, but it was worth the hard work. Come fair week, we were ready.

———————•———————

Equestrians have show moms, the horse equivalent of stage moms. Show Mom arrives at least two hours early to get the best parking spot under the only trees near the ring. That also gives her plenty of time to brush out and touch up the horse, feed and water it, black the hooves, white the socks, and braid the tail. And all before waking the kid, still asleep in the truck. While the kid gets dressed—matching pants and shirt with the big collar and cuffs, big buckle, and a fitted felt hat kept in a box—Show Mom does the kid's hair and makeup, then tacks the horse, bridle, saddle, and a last-minute spit and polish.

There was this one girl, always the prettiest girl with the prettiest horses, best tack, and best clothes. She had shoulder-length hair, but on show days, she had a huge bun on the back of her head. I finally got the nerve to ask how she got her hair so big, and she laughed.

"That old thing? It isn't real. My mom pins a fake bun on my head for show."

Even the prettiest girl with the prettiest horses and all the best stuff had to use fake hair to look right for her Show Mom.

Just before entering the ring, Show Mom props the kid on the horse's back. She watches breathlessly, barking corrections from the rail.

"Sit up straight!

"Your reins are slack!

"The judge is looking right at you!"

Show Mom cheers madly when her kid wins; she clucks and stomps in protest if they don't. Sometimes the horse is to blame, sometimes the judge is biased, but the kid is never wrong.

When class is over, Show Mom meets the kid at the exit gate, takes the horse while the kid jumps down and goofs off until the next class. Show Mom gives her little equestrian a handful of cash to go to the concession stand for a large pop, a hot dog, potato chips, and a candy bar. They take a few bites, a few sips, then leave them on the side of the truck for the flies and the bees.

Mom and Daddy came to our first few shows, but we didn't need anyone to help us get dressed or do our hair. Mom didn't know how to brush or saddle a horse, so she wouldn't have been much help there either.

We were lucky to pick up a few good pieces of tack at yard sales and hand-me-downs from fellow 4-H club members. Finding decent pony-size tack wasn't easy, so we had to cut down a bridle and halter to fit Holly. The buckstitching was plastic, not leather, so it looked cheap and was always dirty. I cleaned it with my toothbrush and tucked in all the broken stitches. I used white paint to fill in any missing stitches. The one new thing I had was a pony-size Western saddle Mom got for $19.95 at a tack shop on US 12. At first glance, it looked like suede, but it was mostly pressed cardboard, so you couldn't trust it in the rain.

What we didn't have, we borrowed from Missy Kjellberg with the promise that we would win blue ribbons and give it back when we had our own. Nothing matched, but we would use Daddy's brown shoe polish to at least try to get them the same color.

"Betty Lou! Where's my goddamned shoe polish?"

Our show "apparel" was just our best school clothes. Catherine borrowed slacks and a polyester blouse from Mary. I wore my best corduroys and a vest over a white turtleneck. My pants were too short, so they rode up my leg, showing my whole boot and sock. Mom used one of her chiffon scarves to tie a dime-store cowboy hat to my head.

Once we got the hang of it, Mom would just drop the trailer and come back for us at the end of the day. We never got smart enough to call a couple hours before we needed picking up, so we were always waiting a couple hours after the show was over. More than once, we were locked in, and Mom would have to drive over to the fairgrounds office to have a groundskeeper open the gate. By that time, we would be pretty hungry, having used all the money she gave us for entry fees and nothing to eat since that morning.

As a kid, I didn't know we weren't equestrians. I didn't understand that we didn't belong. And I didn't know I would spend the rest of my life trying to cover up a murder.

Dear Diary,

I won 2 blue ribbons! At the fair with Holly. She did so good. First we had halter class in the morning. Holly stood perfect. We got a blue ribbon with 6th place.

And then we did riding class in the afternoon. Pee Wee Under Saddle. And for that class we won 1st place!!!!!!!!!! The judge smiled and liked Holly alot. Daddy said he was so proud of me.

I cant wait for next summer to go to more shows and win more ribbons.

Love,

Trisha and Holly

21

Spring 1976

"Patricia Anne, sit still," Mom said.

"But I have to pee," I said.

"You just went twenty minutes ago."

Mom was right, I didn't really have to pee. I was antsy and would rather be running around the fairgrounds instead of being stuck in the auction barn, my little butt freezing on the metal bleachers. But you didn't dare tell my mom you were bored. It was like committing a sin. She would give you dumb games to do, like count people, find every color, or memorize a scripture from the little Bible she kept in her purse.

The Saturday livestock sale starts at nine a.m., with everything from poultry and rabbits to cattle and horses. Just outside the auction arena, vendors set up tables throughout the breezeway with anything from expensive collectibles to cheap plastic toys. On one end was a small coffee shop, a tack shop on the other.

"Do I hear ninety, ninety, ninety, ninety...got ninety here, can I get ninety-five, five, five, gimme ninety-five, now five, who'll give me ninety-five...Here! Somebody gimme a hundred, hunna, hunna, hunna, hundred-dollar bill now,

one hundred dollars now, that's for the sow and piglets, one money, one money..."

"What are you buying, Mom?" Katie Catherine asked.

"I'm not sure yet," Mom answered.

"What are you looking for?" I asked.

"Nothing," Mom answered.

"What do you need?" Catherine asked.

"I'll know it when I see it," Mom answered.

"For the pair now, for the pair, can I get a fifty-dollar bill now, fitty, fitty, fitty..."

"Mom?" I asked.

"Patricia Anne, that's enough," Mom said.

"Can I get a hot chocolate?"

"*Can* you?"

"*May* I get a hot chocolate? Please?" I said. "I'm cold."

"I told you this morning to bundle up," she replied. "It's March, it's still cold. But you had to look cool in your 4-H jacket."

"I know, but..."

"Katie Catherine, go with your sister," Mom said, handing her some change.

"I can go by myself!" I said, grabbing the change. "I'm not a baby."

"Well don't get lost," Mom said. "And come right back."

"OK, OK."

"Trisha?"

"What?"

"Don't you 'what' me, young lady."

"Yes, ma'am."

"Here—leave this catalog on the counter."

Down the steps and out of sight, I turned left toward the vendors instead of right toward the coffee shop. I dropped the catalog in the trash barrel and checked the clock on the wall, giving myself ten minutes to wander the market. So many trinkets, tools, candles, and perfumes. Church ladies' bake sale. Key chains and crocheted mittens on card tables. Expensive antiques and chipped china cups with mismatched saucers.

But mostly I just wanted to get to the tack shop and covet.

There were stacks of saddles and racks of bridles. Used saddles smell like leather and horse sweat. I would bury my face under the fender and take a deep breath. There were shelves and shelves of anything you could want and fancy things you would certainly never need. Halters and bits, cleaners and polish, wormer pastes and healing poultices. I would run my hands over the bristles of brightly colored brushes, soft and coarse. Dab some pricey liniment on my sleeve so I could smell it later.

In the back corner was a rack of ten-gallon hats with gaudy snakeskin hatbands and a spray of feathers on the fronts. The owner lady said, "Can you believe some guy just bought one this morning? Fifty bucks. Hmmph."

When she wasn't looking, I dropped a shiny metal hoof pick in my pocket. If I got caught, I could just say it was already in there. *Oh this? It's my lucky hoof pick.*

By the door was a promotional display of apple-flavored horse treats and a bowl of samples with a sign that said "Take one only please." I lingered, pretending I was very interested, then stuffed two in my pocket and scurried out.

"Hey you!" I heard behind me.

I ducked behind the cinnamon roasted almonds cart, my back against the wheel. There was some of the usual commotion and murmuring in the breezeway. I hid the hoof pick on top of the cart wheel, just in case. *Take what? See? Nothing in my pockets.*

I held my breath, closed my eyes, and crossed my fingers tight. *Pass me by, pass me by, pass me by.*

Footsteps, queries. "Did you see a...?"

Pass me by, pass me by, pass me by.

"Get your almonds here, get your almonds right here now, two for five..."

Exhale. It worked again.

I checked the clock—my ten minutes were well past. I poked my head in the auction arena. Mom was now surrounded by other ladies, talking, looking at Avon catalogs, testing samples. Catherine had moved down to the front row on the fence, closer to the animals. I wasn't missed. Still time to get my hot chocolate.

Inside the coffee shop, the auctioneer call is replaced by diners' chatter, the cold for heat, the smell of dust and manure for coffee and grease. Men in bib overalls turn to look when cold air wafts in the door with you. The menu board is way too big for the few items sold there, including the twenty-five-cent cup of hot chocolate.

Waiting in line, I imagined my impending interrogation and prepared excuses:

1. I went to the bathroom first.
2. There was a line for the bathroom.
3. There was a line at the coffee shop.
4. They were out of hot chocolate and needed to go to the storeroom to get more.

"*What* kind of rinky-dink outfit are y'all runnin' here?" a voice boomed from the front of the line.

The din of chatter in the room hushed, and all heads turned.

Ronnie Clark. There he stood, wearing a brand-new ten-gallon hat with a gaudy snakeskin hatband and a spray of feathers on the front.

"Y'all can't break a hunnert dollar bill?" he barked, waving a fistful of bills around.

"I'm sorry, sir, do you have anything smaller?" asked the old lady behind the register. Her lavender hairnet matched her apron. A button on her collar read "Ask me about my grandkids."

"Lemme see here." He turned his back to her, leaned his elbow on the counter, and leafed through his handful of bills, performing. Sucked his teeth and smiled, showing a gold tooth. "No, ma'am, only hunnerts."

"Well, it's just a twenty-five-cent coffee," the cashier said softly. "You go on and take it."

"Look here, grandma," he snapped, digging in his pocket. "I don't need your fuckin' charity." He slapped some change on the counter, snatched the Styrofoam cup, and stormed out mumbling, "Bunch of dumbass hillbillies…"

The door slammed shut, and chatter resumed. A sign on the back of the door said "Please don't slam the door."

Lavender hairnet was momentarily shaken by the kerfuffle, but by the time it was my turn in line, she and the other hairnets had concluded that he was a jackass. "I'm sorry you had to hear that cussin', sweetie," she said, sliding the Styrofoam cup across the counter to me.

Hot chocolate in hand, I checked the clock: I'd been gone twenty minutes. Pushing through the crowd in the breezeway, I held my hot chocolate with both hands, mentally preparing for interrogation. "There was a long line!" I'd plead. I rounded the corner to the auction arena and *bam*—ran smack-dab into Ronnie Clark.

"What in the hell?" he yelled.

Flat on my back in the dust, I looked up to see him standing over me.

"Watch where you goin' child," he said, reaching down to yank me up by the front of my jacket.

"I-I'm sorry, I didn't mean it. I didn't see you."

"You spilled shit all over my boots," he said, releasing his grip.

"I said I'm sorry," I said, moving around him.

He propped his leg in the doorjamb, blocking my way. "Not so fast, tiger. Look what you did to my boot," he said, pulling up his pant leg. Above the sticky stain on his toe, a bright-orange screaming eagle spread its wings across the shaft.

I ducked under his leg to run, but he caught one of my pigtails, jerking me back against his chest. With my head pulled back, he looked straight down at my face. I could smell his coffee breath and cheap cologne.

"Looks like I caught a little tiger by the tail, didn't I?" His upper lip peeled back over the gold tooth.

"Let me *go!*" I yelled, stomping my heel on his toe.

"Ow, you little bitch!"

I ran straight to Catherine on the other side of the ring. Her arms were stretched through the rails to feel the calves as they walked by.

"*Getta here, getta here, can I getta twenty, twenty, twenty dollars a head here, getta here...*"

"Where's the hot chocolate?" Catherine asked. "I thought we were gonna share it."

"I dropped it," I replied, looking toward the door.

"What's wrong with you? You look like you saw a ghost. And why do you smell like liniment?"

Ronnie Clark stepped into the room, scanning the bleachers. I ducked down.

"What are you doing down there?" Catherine asked.

"Is he still there?" I panted.

"Is who still there?"

"Mr. Clark."

"Yeah, why?"

"He..."

"Last up, folks, for your consideration, this is Churchill, a two-year-old Hereford bull from Umholtz Farms. Nice dark red, goggled ring eye. He's stout and growthy. He weaned at seven hundred fifty pounds with a yearling weight of eleven hundred pounds. Health papers are up to date today. Bud Umholtz tells me he's out of their best cow and he's showy but docile, he'll load in your trailer with just a bucket of grain. Let's get this started at three hundred dollars, can I get a three, three, three, who'll give me three, here's three now, three..."

"Hey, kiddo, you lost one of your ponytail holders," Catherine said. "Your braid's falling out."

Reflexively, I reached for my braid, now unraveled up to my ear and curled at the bottom. I peeked through the railing across the pen and saw Ronnie Clark standing in the door.

Churchill moved around the ring as if he was looking for an out, an escape. He checked the whole fence and went to the gate, throwing his head up and down. This close, I could see the whites of his eyes. He swished his long downy tail; the curls smacked the rail at my face.

"Be careful, girls, he's dangerous," the auctioneer warned. "C'mon and get back from the fence there."

Catherine and I stepped back and sat on the lowest bleacher, stung by the scolding from a stranger.

"Is Mom looking?" Catherine asked.

Turning slowly to peek over my shoulder, I found Mom's eyes locked on us. Arms crossed, she was shaking her head disapprovingly.

"Nope," I lied. "She's talking to another lady."

"Good."

"Churchill doesn't seem mean to me. Just scared."

"Sometimes when animals are scared is when they're the most dangerous."

"Maybe people are the same way, huh?"

"Maybe," Catherine said. "So what were you doing out there? Look—you're all dirty, your braid is out, you're sweaty, your face is all red. Mom's gonna..."

"We're at three forty, forty, forty, forty, now fifty, somebody gimme three fifty, now fifty, thank you, ma'am, who's with me at three sixty, that's a bargain now, not even forty cent a pound... come on now, gimme three sixty, sixty, sixty now, sixty, bid three sixty, you sir...?"

"What did you do?" Catherine asked. She knelt down and took my shoulders. "Trisha? Did you get in trouble again? Why do you smell like liniment? Did you steal...?"

"Three, three, three, now three seventy-five, do I hear eighty, three eighty, three hundred eighty dollars now, would you give three eighty, sir? Fair warning now, last call now at three seventy-five, he's yours in the back at three seventy-five, going once, going twice..."

"*Five* hundred!" a voice boomed from the doorway. The room clucked, groaned, and snickered. Farmers in the stands craned their necks to see who had made the foolish bid. Surely it's a joke, right?

"Ahem, uh, who's there? Whose bid was that?" asked the auctioneer.

"That's *my* bid," Ronnie Clark said, stepping to the front. His hat entered before he did.

"Well alright, sir, but we were at three eighty. Did you say five hundred?"

"That's right, I said *five* hunnert. What? You don't think I got it? Look here," he said, waving his wad of bills.

"Who's he trying to impress?" someone hissed from the stands.

"Show-off."

"Asshole."

"Proverbs says a fool has money in his hand but he has no sense," Catherine said.

"Bidder in the back? The bid's at five hundred. Do I hear five hundred ten?" the auctioneer said.

"The hell I will. Let him have the damned thing."

"Yeah, that's right," Ronnie Clark said, laughing, looking around for support that was not there.

"Sold! For five hundred dollars to bidder number...uh, what's your number, Mister uh...?"

"It's Clark. Ronnie Clark. And my number is five hundred," he boasted, fanning out his bills.

The crowd spilled out into the breezeway. Small clusters of conversation congealed here and there but left a buffer around Ronnie Clark, like a drop of oil in water. The line to the office was long but moving quickly as people paid for their purchases. Mom struck up a conversation with the people around her in line. I tugged at her shirt to get her attention—"Mom, Mom, Mom"—but she ignored me.

"Mom, can I go wait in the car?" I asked, keeping my head on a swivel.

"No, the last time you did that, you got lost in the horse barns, and I couldn't find you for an hour," Mom said. "And what's that smell?"

"Please, Mom, I—"

"I said no," she snapped. "Where's your sister?"

Ronnie Clark stepped out of the office, counting his bills and making a grand gesture of stuffing them in his breast pocket and snapping the mother-of-pearl snap. I ducked behind Mom, waiting for him to pass, but his fancy boots stopped in front of her.

"Hello, Ron," Mom said.

"Ma'am," he said, tipping his hat awkwardly, performatively. Like he'd seen it in a movie.

"So, you're starting a beef herd?" she asked.

"Naw, I just don't go home empty-handed."

"How is your family? I've been meaning to stop by—"

"You do that, Miz White," he said, stepping away.

"It's Mrs."

Catherine came out of the bathroom as Mom stepped into the office. I waved to her, but she trotted off down the breezeway—to the horse barns, I figured. I watched her dark curly head disappear in and out of the crowd and reappear in the bright light of the open doorway at the other end. She stood facing a tall man in a big hat. Their silhouettes looked like an old-timey shadow show. Her face was turned up toward his, he bent with his hands on his knees. His hat covered both their heads like an umbrella. As they broke, she lifted her hand to shake his. He put his hand on her side and waved her back to us.

———•———

"Mom? Remember how you said I could start babysitting to make some money?" Katie Catherine asked from the back seat on our way home from the auction.

"Yes, mm-hmm."

"Well, what if it wasn't babysitting? What if it was barn work for a neighbor?"

"What are you talking about?"

"Well, Karen and Mary get all the babysitting jobs because they're older."

"Mm-hmm."

"Well, what if I clean stalls and stuff for Mr. Clark to make some money? Instead of babysitting."

"You're twelve years old, Katie Catherine," Mom said. "Too young for a job."

"Dan was younger than her when he started working," I said.

"You watch that sass, young lady," Mom said.

"But, Mom, it's the same chores I do in our barn every day," Kate said. "Except I'd get paid for it."

"Working at home is not the same as working for someone else."

"Mom, you had us work for the Kjellbergs last summer," I piped up. "For free."

Pause.

"You won't be able to do your own chores and his," Mom said.

"I did my chores and Dan's chores when he was on the road with Daddy that time."

"I don't want it to interfere with your schoolwork."

"We don't have school over spring break. Can't I try it for just one week?"

"I don't want you down there with those people. Those boys seem pretty wild."

"Well, I don't have to talk to them."

Pause.

"Mom, please. I want to get a job to buy stuff for the horses. For me and Trisha."

"Don't say 'me and Trisha.' It's 'Trisha and me,'" Mom corrected.

"For Trisha and me," she repeated.

I rubbed my fingers across the pilfered hoof pick in my pocket, soliciting a tinge of the rush from before.

"Well, I don't think it's a good idea," Mom said.

"Please, Mom?"

"And I can help with her chores at home," I added.

Pause.

She sighed heavily. "Let me talk to your father about it."

As we pulled in the driveway, Catherine reached into her pocket. "What's this? How did this get here?"

"What is it?" I asked.

"It's your ponytail holder."

22

---•---

If It Was Gone

I never told Katie Catherine, but I missed her terribly when she was gone.

She would spring up early in the morning, do her chores, and be gone before I even woke up. That meant I had to do my chores without shadowing her. All my questions and dreams would have to wait until she got home at night, when they would all spill out of me like a knocked-over teapot.

Despite Mom's concern, Catherine kept up her chores and homework, so spring break work stretched into some weekends. The older kids had sports and jobs, so when she was working, I was on my own. I would ride Holly over to my best friend Becky Lynn's house and ask if she could come out riding with me. Most days, she was allowed to unless she was grounded or had to go somewhere with her family. And some days, her dad was just in a bad mood and wouldn't let her come outside.

Becky Lynn had two families: the one when her dad was around and the one when he wasn't. When he was around, her mom was quiet and in the other room—whatever other room he wasn't in. She would set the table for supper, and every time, he would take his plate and eat in his recliner that no one else was allowed to sit in, even when he wasn't there. Watching the TV that only he could choose the channel with the antenna box on top that only he could adjust. Becky Lynn and her big sister Kimmy knew they had to keep it down in the house in case he was either napping or watching TV. If they did anything outside, they knew they had to stay off his meticulously manicured lawn. I learned the rules the hard way with a "Get that goddamned pony off my lawn before she tears it up!"

When Mr. Grosvenor wasn't around, the three of them came to life. The whole house came to life. They would have friends over, always joking and laughing, singing, telling stories, making cookies together, and doing each other's hair. They were kind to each other, saying things like "Mom, do you need a refill on your sweet tea?" or "Becky Lynn, that color looks good on you." And they hosted the absolute best, most epic slumber parties, complete with truth or dare; ghost stories; pillow forts; pillow fights; light as a feather, stiff as a board; scavenger hunts; Ouija board; pizza; popcorn; Rice Krispies Treats; and root beer floats.

———•———

But I still missed Katie Catherine.

When summer break started, she was sometimes gone all day, so Mom sent me down to the Clarks' with a sack lunch for her. When I got to the driveway, before I could even dismount, the Clark boys were on me out of nowhere.

"Whuddyou want, girl?" Boy Number One said.

"I…uh…I brought my sister's lunch," I said, holding up the bag.

"Shee-it. Huh. Lunch."

They laughed and jabbed each other in the ribs with their elbows. Another joke I was too little to understand, I assumed.

"Whut's yer name, girl?" asked Boy Number Two.

"Trisha."

"Trisha? What kinda name is that?" asked Two.

"Shee-it," added One. "Kinda stupid."

Laugh, laugh. Jab, jab.

"Where'd you get that pony, huh?" Two said. "That's about the ugliest pony I ever seen."

Laugh, laugh. Jab, jab.

"Yeah, that's…that pony's so ugly, he should be called Elmer. Elmer's glue!" added One.

Laugh, laugh. Jab, jab.

"It's a *girl*, and her name is *Holly*!" I huffed.

"Trisha!" Catherine yelled from the barn door. "C'mon. I'm in here."

Keeping a stink eye on the Clark boys, I headed to the barn. "And she is *not* ugly!" I yelped. "*You're* ugly."

Ronnie Clark had two barns on his property. The smaller barn by the house was used as storage for feed and equipment. It had fresh green paint and electricity. The lower slats were set with half-inch gaps to keep hay and grain dry but keep rain out. The big red barn was set way back from the road. Just like ours, it was open in the center with high hay lofts on each side. He'd built out horse stalls and strung an acre of fence for a paddock.

Besides Churchill the bull, he bought some Thoroughbred horses from a local breeder, Eleanor Sjogren. She sold him two high-strung, squirrelly mares and an older stallion, Admiral. He was a gorgeous silver-gray dapple with a pearl-white mane and tail. Admiral was a many-time grand champion and had qualified for nationals, but he was too hard to handle, so she put him out to stud. Here at the Clarks', he thrashed around in his stall and threw himself against the fence of his dinky paddock. Seeing him there was like seeing Baryshnikov at a bus station.

Katie and I sat under a tree at the side of the barn while she ate her lunch. She shared her cookies with me, and I shared them with Holly, tied to the tree and contentedly munching the tall grass. Mrs. Clark had the kitchen window open, and we could hear her singing "Someone to Watch Over Me" while she did dishes.

A lamb in the wood…

Always be good…

To the one who'll watch over me

"What work are you doing today?" I asked.

"I already mucked the stalls," she said. "So now I just have to clean up the small barn, stack the bales and grain sacks."

"Want me to help you finish?" I asked, following her into the barn. "So you can come home quicker?"

"Nah. Not much left to do. But if you want to hang out here until I'm done, I'll walk home with you."

Oh, how I need someone to watch over me

Inside the small barn, rich green alfalfa bales were stacked next to sacks of grain. A pile of sawdust took up a whole corner. On the wall by the door were heavy iron contraptions with chains and jagged toothy edges. They didn't look like any farm equipment I had seen before. Under them were some wooden crates filled with white boxes that looked like laundry detergent. They had a skull and crossbones on the label.

"*Trisha*, get away from that!" Catherine snapped.

"What is all this stuff?"

"Those are his traps, and that's poison. It's dangerous. Don't even touch it."

"What are traps for?"

"He…Never mind. Just get away from that stuff."

Hanging from the last trap was a tail—a long fluffy reddish-brown tail with a white tip at the end. Behind it were two more, only smaller.

"Hey, kiddo," Catherine said. "Do me a favor and go in the tack room and grab me the broom." She pointed to the squared-off room in the corner. "Go ahead, the door should be unlocked."

The walls were solid wood paneling. Cedar. Real wood. Not like the fake stuff in our bedroom. On one side hung double-tiered saddle racks with both Western and English saddles. Stacks of brand-new lambswool saddle pads sat on the floor. On the other wall, tack racks, each one of them doubled and tripled up, were chock-full of new bridles, halters, bits, reins, and leads, many still with price tags. Every one was nicer than the next, some with buckstitching, some with engravings, leather stamps, brass hardware, and a whole lot of silver. Silver bangles, silver plates, silver buckles. Silver on the pommels and skirts and horns of the saddles and on the stirrups. Even the tips of the reins had silver clips.

"Whoa!" I marveled. "Did you see all this stuff?"

"Yeah. He's got some nice tack alright."

"How come he doesn't use it? It's still got price tags on it."

"I don't know. I've never even seen him ride."

On the floor was a large trunk, painted hunter green.

"What's in here?" I called out. "This big green box?"

"I don't know. Quit snooping around. I don't want Mr. Clark to catch us going through his stuff."

Of course I opened it. Under a pile of brand-spanking-new blankets was a tangle of new brushes, currycombs, hoof picks, hoof black, and leg wraps. Everything was just dumped. And at the bottom of the trunk, I found a headstall with mold growing on one side.

"Did you see this?" I asked, holding up the bridle.

"No, what about it?"

"It's all moldy."

"Oh, OK. Just hang it up over there, and I'll get to it tomorrow."

The very idea of having tack you don't use or take care of was alien to me. To us. We cleaned and oiled every item we owned. Dusty's show halter was the nicest thing we had. It was real leather with fake white buckstitching. After cleaning and oiling the leather, Catherine would have to go back over the plastic buckstitching with a Q-tip. Every bit of it was a pleasure for us. A ritual.

"I bet he doesn't even remember he has it," I said.

"Yeah, probly not," Catherine said.

Pause.

"I bet he wouldn't even miss it. If it was gone."

"Probly not."

Pause.

"I bet we could take a lot of stuff, and he wouldn't even miss it."

"Probly not."

Pause.

"I bet—"

"Trisha, we are *not* taking any of his stuff, so don't even think about it!"

"But you said yourself he doesn't even use it and wouldn't even know it was gone."

"That doesn't make it right to steal! Stealing is a sin."

"But is it really stealing, though, if he's not even using it?" I asked, holding up an armload of new halters with price tags still hanging on them.

"Stealing is stealing, and stealing is wrong." She punctuated *wrong* by stabbing the pitchfork into a pile of alfalfa.

Pause.

"What if we just borrow it for a while? And bring it back before he notices?"

"Trisha, no. We're *not* taking anything. For*get* it."

"What if we just borrow one small thing, wait to see if he notices?" Lifting a currycomb, I pitched my voice a little higher to soften the sinful suggestion.

Pause.

"Mom would kill us if she caught us stealing."

"But look at this one." I picked up one of the many bridles, this one with real leather buckstitching on each side and a silver plate on the browband. "That would look pretty on Dusty."

From the wall, we heard a thump and a squeal. I could see Holly through the slats on that side, shifting around. Another thump and another squeal.

"Holly!" I yelled and ran out the door.

I assumed it was a horsefly getting to her where she couldn't swat it, but then I saw One and Two ducking in and out of the cornfield, chucking rocks at her. I got there just in time to see one bounce off her rump.

"Hey!" I yelled, running to shield her. "Quit it, you buttholes!"

They ran into the cornstalks, laughing.

"It's OK, Holly," I said, untying her. "It's OK, girl." Hot tears hit my cheeks. "Buttholes!" I yelled into the corn.

"C'mon, bring her in the barn and let's check her over," Catherine said. "Make sure she's OK."

"I'm telling Mom!" I cried, wiping snot on my sleeve. Holding Holly's halter, I stroked her neck and kissed her forehead while Catherine methodically inspected her for wounds. "I mean it…I'm telling Mom, and she'll tell Mr. Clark, and those boys"—*sniffle*—"they're gonna get it, like before."

"She's OK," Catherine said, patting her round rump. "Just a little shook up."

"I wish they would die. I wish they would get run over by a tractor and die."

"Don't wish bad things, Trisha. Take it back. God can hear you."

"Good! Did God see them throwing rocks at Holly? Doesn't God punish people for being bad too?"

"You let God worry about them."

"I'll tell Daddy! He'll—"

"Please don't tell Daddy. She's OK."

"But Daddy likes Holly. He'll—"

"If you tell Daddy, I won't be able to work here anymore. And I won't get enough money for us to get stable blankets."

"Stable blankets?"

"Yep. If I make enough, I'll get stable blankets for Dusty and Holly to wear to shows this year."

"Really?"

"Yep. Really."

"Well…how much money do you have to make?"

"A lot. Almost a hundred dollars."

A loud whistle rang out from the big barn.

"That's Mr. Clark," Catherine said. "I'll go see what he wants. You and Holly stay put, and I'll be right back. I mean it—stay in here. Don't you go looking for those boys. And don't let her poop on the floor in here. I just got it clean. When I come back, I'll finish up and walk you home."

Holly had her eye set on the alfalfa bales stacked in the corner, so I let her at them. While she indulged, I put my arms around her and laid my head on her withers while the last of my crying subsided.

"Stupid boys," I said. "I don't care if God can hear me. Or Santa. I *do* wish they would die. I wish God would run over them with *ten* tractors. Buttholes."

I picked up the moldy bridle, looking toward the door. Catherine and Mr. Clark were around the back of the house, their long late-afternoon shadows stretching to the top of the driveway.

Oh, how I need someone to watch over me

When Catherine got back to the barn, Holly and I were gone, and the moldy bridle was hanging on a nail outside the tack room.

Nothing else seemed out of place.

Dear God,

Thank you for answering my prayers to have a job so I can earn money. Through God all things are possible. So far I have earned $22 dollars.

Mr. Clark's work is different than my chores at home. Something new every day. Stacking hay, cleaning stalls, clean the water tanks. I helped him fix a fence and hit my thumb with the hammer. Admiral the stallion keeps kicking the fence so we have to fix it good. He is more wild than Dusty!

God, with Your grace, I am learning how to talk to Mr. Clark's dogs. They are Doberman pinchers. They are not bad dogs they just look scary. They like being petted. They are smarter then Sarge and McKeever.

Amen
Katie Catherine

Proverbs 23:4-5
Genesis 1:24-25

Red, White, and Blue

"Mom, what's a bicentennial?" I asked.

"Go look it up," she answered.

Once the big kids were in high school, Mom invested in a set of World Book encyclopedias—the original internet—to help with homework. They were bound in black and brown faux leather covers, proudly displayed on a bookshelf in the dining room. And since I peppered her with questions about everything from aardvarks to Zambonis, she used the encyclopedias as armor. To every question, she could deflect me with a simple "Go look it up."

Before I could even pull down the B volume, Dan barked, "It's America's two hundredth birthday, dummy."

"Nuh-uh," I said. "How can America have a birthday?"

The whole country was swept up in a tsunami of patriotism and nostalgia. Every day on the news, there was another celebration here and observance there, a new statue there and tribute to a battle here. There were covered wagons and a freedom train crossing the country. Everywhere you looked, the bicentennial flag flew with the American flag, and fire hydrants and post office boxes were painted red, white, and blue. We had special stamps, coins, and license plates.

And every damn product on the shelves—cereal, beer, potato chips, paper plates, Zippo lighters, sneakers, comic books, pinball machines, lawn mowers, cars, you name it—if it could be marketed in red, white, and blue, it was.

We watched the Summer Olympics on TV and cheered on the Americans in every sport. Karen and Mary swooned over Bruce Jenner. "He's such a hunk!" they would say. But the star of the show for me was Russian gymnast Olga Korbut. Daddy said she was a Commie, but I loved her little ponytails and bangs.

"Mom, can I cut my hair like that?" I asked.

"Absolutely not," Mom said. "You're too young for short hair, and you wouldn't take care of it. Besides, I love your pigtails. You look like Pippi Longstocking."

Our school curriculum for the entire year was based on the bicentennial. We learned about the Boston Tea Party, the Revolutionary War, and the Declaration of Independence. Our school participated in countywide bicentennial beauty pageants, softball tournaments, and poster contests. Everyone had to write an essay about what it means to be an American.

The celebration was a palate cleanser after the Vietnam War and the Watergate scandal. From a kid's perspective, we had a general feeling that everything was gonna be OK—a collective exhale. Our ancestors and parents had fought all the wars that would ever be fought and built all the roads and bridges we would ever need. Hell, they even walked on the moon. All we had to do was enjoy it. Everything was in front of us: peace, prosperity, cloning, flying cars, and jet packs.

24

•

July 3, 1976

Our 4-H club had been preparing for the bicentennial Fourth of July parade for months. WCSR, the local radio station, was giving a fifty-dollar prize to the best dressed group, and we were going for it. We had four Founding Fathers, six Revolutionary soldiers, one Martha Washington, and two Paul Reveres. The rest of us were just decked out in red, white, and blue from our hatbands to the ribbons in our horses' tails. Mom made matching flag vests for Catherine and me.

The night before the parade, we were in the barn, cleaning and prepping tack. Catherine was cleaning Dusty's bridle when the buckle on the headstall gave out again, the prong falling in the dust at her feet.

"Dang it!" Catherine said. "I don't know how many more times I can fix this thing. Can you get me some binder twine and scissors?"

"Sure." In the tack room, I picked around for the scissors, pilfered from Mom's sewing stuff.

"Where are my Fiskars?" she would yell from another room. "Which one of you kids took my Fiskars? These are not toys! These are not for playing with—they are very expensive." Then she'd mumble something about how she can never have nice things.

Catherine managed to fix the bridle but couldn't hide the twine. "That looks pretty hillbilly," she said. "Can you find a little piece of wire?"

"Sure."

When I came back, I lowered a brand-new bridle onto her lap. Tanned leather with real buckstitching on each side and a silver plate on the browband.

"What's this?" she asked.

"A new bridle."

"Where did you get it?" she asked, looking around. "It's not my birthday."

Pause.

"I took it."

"You what?"

"I borrowed it."

"Wait…this is Mr. Clark's!"

I nodded.

"You took it?"

I nodded.

"When? How?"

"Remember that day I brought you lunch? And helped you clean the tack barn?"

"Ugh…I told you not to take anything!"

"I know, but—"

"But what? This is stealing, Trisha."

"But he has so much, and he doesn't use it, and…well, we need it."

"That doesn't make it right. It's still stealing. It's a sin."

"Sorry."

"Well, I have to take this back. Hopefully he hasn't noticed it's gone."

"He hasn't noticed. It's been gone for months."

"Trisha, that's a sin."

"Won't hurt to use it for the parade, right?"

"I can't do that."

"If you take it back, it's not stealing, just borrowing."

"It's not borrowing if you didn't ask permission."

"No one will know, and you'll put it back before anyone does know."

"It's still a sin."

"Seems like more of a sin to flash your money all around and brag and buy all that nice stuff just to leave it to rot in his barn."

"That's for God to judge."

For more than a few minutes, we stood holding the bridle, touching the stitching, studying the silver plate, running the long supple reins through our fingers.

"It's real pretty, isn't it?" I said.

"Trisha, I'm *not* using it tomorrow," she said. "It's wrong."

"Yeah," I said.

"It couldn't hurt to just try it on him though, right?" she asked. She adjusted the buckle and slipped it over Dusty's head.

Sun caught the silver band on his forehead, flashing us in the eyes. If you didn't know better, you'd never know the bit in his mouth was worth more than the whole horse.

"Looks good on him," I said.

"Yeah, it does," she said.

2 5

•

July 4, 1976

We didn't win the fifty dollars.

Other groups had covered wagons full of pioneer ladies in bonnets, Uncle Sams on stilts, and Lady Liberties driving John Deere tractors. One of our competitors took it up a notch, performing a war reenactment between revolutionaries and redcoats in full costume. Another group had a team of Clydesdales pulling a boat on wheels, depicting Washington crossing the Delaware. It was quite the spectacle for Hillsdale County.

Karen and Mary marched with the cheerleaders, and Dan was driving the tractor pulling the school float. Catherine and I had fun waving at all the people and tossing peppermints to the kids at the edge of the crowd. Mom and Daddy were in the bleachers, smiling and waving, taking pictures.

No one even noticed Dusty's new bridle.
Or so we thought.

26

Not a Word

Betty Lou wasn't the type of parent to defend her children from accusation or punishment. Quite the contrary. Unlike parents today, if any adult accused one of her children of doing something wrong, she figured they were probably right. You'll recall she told all our teachers they had her permission to beat her children if they needed to. "Where there's smoke, there's fire" was her philosophy.

She would have believed Ronnie Clark too. She didn't like him, but she would have believed him because he's an adult. She would have believed that Catherine had stolen his stuff, and she would have been judge, jury, and hangman right there in the driveway. Right there in front of Ronnie Clark. And Catherine would have taken the heat for me if she could, but she was a terrible liar. Betty Lou would have seen through her lie and homed right in on me, the known thief. I would have been interrogated until I broke down crying and confessed. I would have returned the loot, right there in the driveway. The whole transaction would have taken ten minutes. We would have been soundly punished. Maybe spanked. Definitely grounded.

I would have fessed up.

But he used the f-word before I had the chance.

Catherine and I had been out riding and stopped at the house to get some Kool-Aid, tying Dusty and Holly to the railing while we ran inside. When we came out, we saw his pickup in the drive-way and Mom and Ronnie Clark face-to-face in front of it, talking.

"Look, I was nice enough to hire your kid and pay her."

"What did she do?"

"She's been stealing shit from my barn!" he said, gesturing toward us.

"What? That doesn't sound like my Katie Catherine," Mom said. "Catherine, come here right now."

We both walked over, still holding our plastic Tupperware tumblers full of Kool-Aid, eyes wide. *Oh, boy. Here it comes.*

"Catherine Marguerite, did you steal from Mr. Clark?"

"I…uh…well, I…" She looked at me.

"Don't look at her," Mom said. "You look at me and tell me the truth. Did you steal from Mr. Clark?"

"I…uh," Catherine said.

I had to confess. I couldn't let my sister lie for me, and I couldn't let her take the fall for what I had done. I took a deep breath and—

"Don't you lie now," Ronnie Clark said, wagging his bony finger in her face. "Fuckin' stealing my tack, right out of my own fuckin' barn. She's using it right now! That's my fuckin' bridle!" he said, pointing at Dusty.

Cue record scratch.

Mom gasped audibly, clutched her chest, and shifted her glare from Catherine to Ronnie Clark. Time stopped, and the oxygen went out of the air.

"Mr. Clark! Why, I never…" she exclaimed. "How *dare* you talk that way in front of me!" Turning to shield us, she added, "And in front of children! In front of little girls!"

At that point, we could have been guilty as sin. Caught red-handed, lock-'em-up-and-throw-away-the-key guilty, and she would have defended us. We could have been standing there, draped in stolen loot, reeking of leather and silver polish, and we would have been innocent in her eyes. Because to my mother, there was no greater crime than saying the f-word in her presence.

If he just hadn't said *fuck*, none of this would have happened. It's not even that it's a cuss word. If adequately provoked, Mom would occasionally cuss—usually yelling at us kids. But there was one word that she never used and never tolerated. Not in print or movies, and especially not in her presence. The f-word.

Even if it wasn't directed at her, if it was within earshot, it was a personal affront to her. You had insulted her both as a person and as a lady. Once you let that one fly, you lost all credibility. In her mind, if you could do that, well, there was really no telling what you wouldn't do. You had disrespected her, so you did not deserve her respect. It was not a word; it was a violation.

"You girls go on now," she said, stern but calm, never taking her eyes off Ronnie Clark.

Tugging at her shirt, I said, "But Mommy, I—"

"I said go!" she snapped. "Right now!"

We must have looked like one of those scenes from Westerns when the dudes hop on their horses outside a saloon and hightail it down a dusty street. By the time we got to a good spot in the barn to watch what was going on, he was getting in his truck. Words were still being exchanged, but we couldn't make out what was being said. He peeled out, dust swirling behind him. As a final insult, he gave her the finger out the sliding back window of his truck as he sped down the road.

————————•————————

Daddy was on the road, so we didn't have family supper that night and could stay at the barn until well after dark. Finally, we were hungry and ready to face the music. When we got in the house, Mom was on the phone, talking to one of her customers. We made sandwiches and ate them in front of the TV, still waiting for what we had coming to us. When she hung up, Mom went about her business like nothing had happened.

Nothing was said until the next night. Daddy was home, so Mom made a big family supper. "How's your job with Mr. Clark going?" Daddy asked.

Catherine and I stopped chewing and looked at Mom. Had she told him what had happened?

Before Catherine could answer, Mom said, "She's not working for him anymore. I don't care for his kind. He has a filthy mouth."

"Well, be that as it may, Betty Lou, I need to talk to him about his hay elevator," Daddy said. "See if he'll let us use it to put hay up this year."

"Can't we use the Kjellbergs'?" Mom asked.

"Darryl said his boys'll be needing it. Ron has one. I'll ask him."

Catherine kicked me under the table. We knew Ronnie Clark would tell Daddy about the stolen stuff. Telling Daddy was worse than telling Mom.

Daddy could not be put off by the f-word.

27

What If

"Kate?" I whispered.

No answer.
"Katie Catherine," I repeated.
No answer.
I waited for her to finish her prayers.
"I already prayed about it," she said. "First thing tomorrow, I'm gonna give the stuff back, tell him I'm sorry, and take my licks for it."

"That's not fair. You didn't take it, I did."

"I didn't have to go along with it. I didn't have to use it. I knew better. Now I'm just as guilty."

"Then I'll go with you."

"No way. If Mom finds out I let you do it, I'll be in twice as much trouble."

"You didn't let me do it, I did it on my own."

"Trisha, that doesn't matter, don't you get it? You're little, so when you're with me, I'm responsible for what you do. Can't you understand that?"

Karen poked her head in the door. "Will you two shut up!"

"Yeah, go to sleep," Mary piped in from their room.

183

"Sit on it, Mary, and mind your own beeswax!" I barked back.

"You girls keep it down up there!" Daddy bellowed from the bottom of the steps. "You don't want me to have to come up there, do you?"

"No, Daddy."

"Kate?" I whispered.

"Go to sleep!" she hissed back.

"What if we could give it back without fessin' up?" I asked.

"Go. To. Sleep."

I climbed up to her bunk and sat cross-legged at her feet. "If you fess up to Ronnie Clark, he *will* tell Mom," I said.

"So, I'll tell her first."

"Tell her what? That you stole it? You can't lie to Mom. You can't lie because God won't let you."

Catherine had a tell when she lied. She could not look the person in the eye, and her right knee would shake. She believed it was God's hand, keeping her from committing the sin of lying.

"Just hear me out," I said. "I have a plan."

28

·

There the Whole Time

Catherine taught me everything. But she had a lot to learn about how to undo a theft.

Months earlier, the older kids had gone to the movies, and I had gotten into Karen's makeup bag. I was careful to note exactly how it was placed in the bathroom vanity drawer so I could return it without her knowing I had touched it. It was my intention to return it before they got home, but I fell asleep in a pile of coloring books on the living room floor.

They spilled into the house, still laughing about the movie.
Don't slam the door!
Slam.

I woke with a start, realizing right away that I hadn't put the makeup back. I quickly shoved it under the couch and pretended to be asleep.

"Hey, kiddo, you sleeping?" Dan said, tousling my hair.

"Yeah."

Don't say 'yeah,' dear.

"What do you have all over your hands?" Mary asked.

"What? Where?" I stammered.

"There." She pointed. "It looks like blue eyeshadow."

"Were you in my makeup again?" Karen asked sternly.

"No," I answered. "It's crayon."

"Crayon?" Karen questioned. "What's that on your cheek?"

Before I could answer, she turned on her heel and yelled, "Mom! Trisha's been in my makeup again!"

Anticipating a conflict, Dan and Mary cleared out.

Minutes later, Karen emerged from the kitchen and went into the bathroom, slamming drawers. Back out she came, threw a menacing glare in my direction, said, "You're gonna get it," and stomped up the stairs.

I stuffed the makeup bag under my shirt and hurried to the bathroom. Running the water to muffle the sound, I pulled the vanity drawer all the way out and put the makeup bag way in the back, behind the troop of hairbrushes, rattail combs, and barrettes. I flushed the toilet for cover, washed my hands out of habit, and hurried back to my coloring books on the floor.

Wiping her hands on her apron, Mom emerged from the kitchen. "Trisha darlin'," she said. "Were you in your sister's things again? You know you're not supposed to get into her things."

"No, Mom," I responded.

She picked up my freshly washed hands, examining them closely.

"Maybe she just forgot where she put it," I offered. "Maybe it moved when she opened the drawers."

"We'll see," she said, looking suspicious. Mom went to the bathroom. One drawer opened and closed. Another drawer opened, hairbrushes shuffled around, the drawer closed. "Karen!" Mom yelled. "Get down here."

"What?" Karen said as she tromped down the stairs.

"Don't you 'what' me, young lady," Mom said.

"Yes, ma'am," Karen said.

Mom held out the makeup bag. "Is this what you were looking for?"

"Yes," Karen responded, looking around Mom at me. "See, I *told* you she had it!"

"It was in the bathroom, in your drawer," Mom said.

"But…she…" She pointed at my hands, now washed clean of evidence.

"She's been right there, coloring, all night," Mom said, walking back to the kitchen.

"See? It was there the whole time," I said. "You just weren't looking in the right place."

Dear God,

I know You are testing my faith in You.

And I will pass the test.

And I will bring her to You.

She is like that lost lamb but she steals stuff.

And the Devil made me go along with it.

We will make this right God.

Amen,
Katie Catherine

Proverbs 17:17

29

Chk-Chk

"Trisha, wake up," Catherine whispered, standing next to my bed. "It's time."

It was a typical night in most ways—chores, dinner, watching TV in the living room. One by one, everyone went to bed, and I fell asleep on the living room floor. Around midnight, Daddy nudged me with his foot and told me to go up to bed. No one noticed anything out of the ordinary. No one noticed that Catherine and I left our boots outside and went to bed in our barn clothes. And no one knew I had a pilfered frozen steak under my pillow.

In the dark, Catherine removed our bedroom window screen and motioned for me to climb out. As I lowered myself down to the TV antenna—conveniently located right outside our bedroom window—she held one finger to her lips and said, "Shh." She followed and pulled the screen back into place behind her. Mom and Daddy's bedroom window was inconveniently located right below ours, and because it was summer, that window was dangerously open. We moved slowly and stealthily until we reached the ground. In our stocking feet, we picked up our boots from the side porch and crept around the back of the house and down to the barn. We pulled on our boots, grabbed a grain sack with the stolen bridle in it, and headed out.

When we reached Daddy's garage, Sarge and McKeever trotted up alongside us.

"Dang it, Sarge, git!" Catherine snapped. "Go on, git!" She pointed back toward the house.

"You get the flashlight, and I'll take care of the dogs," I said.

When she ducked in the side door of the garage, I pulled out the frozen steak, peeled off the cellophane, let the dogs sniff it, then threw it as far as I could into the field. "Go get it!"

The dogs were bounding into the field when Catherine came out of the garage with Daddy's big silver flashlight. "What did you do?" she asked.

"Threw a stick," I lied.

"Hmmph, that's weird. I've never seen them play fetch."

"Really? That is weird."

We took our time, scuffing our feet and stomping in puddles. The moon was near full and very bright that night. I pulled the tops off roadside milkweed and blew the fluffy white seeds in the air. Catherine shared the peppermints she had in her pocket. At the bridge, we stopped to throw stones in the creek—or "crick," as we called it. We took turns throwing rocks at the moon's reflection on the water, smashing it like a big china plate, the broken pieces rippling on the water before settling back into place.

Back on the road, we heard a bark and stopped in our tracks.

"Dang it," she said. "McGee's dogs."

Standing between us and our destination was the McGee family property. Stretching for a hundred yards with multiple mobile homes, barns, and outbuildings, it looked more like a compound. And scattered from one end to the other were at least a dozen twitchy mutts chained to rickety dog houses.

We stood silent. I watched Catherine's face to gauge the situation.

"Maybe we should just go home," she said.

"We can't," I said. "We gotta get this stuff back before we get in trouble."

"How?" she asked. "We can't get past these dogs."

"What if we go around the block?" I said.

"That would take too long. Sun would be coming up by the time we got there."

I looked at my watch with the flashlight. "It's two thirty now."

She looked at the dogs, then back toward home, then back at the dogs. "We're gonna have to make a run for it," Catherine said. "Take off your boots. Carry 'em. Run on the soft side so you don't make too much noise. They're still gonna bark, but we can get past 'em before anyone wakes up."

"You think that'll work?" I asked.

"Yeah, they'll just think it was a possum."

We pulled off our boots and each took a deep breath.

"Ready?" she asked.

"Yep."

Here's something you may not know: on the side of every country road is a narrow trough of the softest silty sand. When rain flows across fields, it leaves clay and heavy soil behind and deposits the sand at the edge of the road, like a thin strip of tropical beach, totally out of place.

We ran. Catherine went first, and I stayed as close behind as I could, focused on her striped shirt in front of me. The dogs broke out in a frenzy of barking before we got halfway past the property. When I looked over my shoulder as we cleared the property line, a porch light came on.

"Whew! We made it!" I whispered, panting.

"Yeah!" Catherine said.

"Did you see the light come on? I thought we were goners."

"Nah, we're too fast. I told you they'd just think the dogs are barking at a possum or something."

The dogs continued barking. *Ruff, ruff! Ruff, ruff!*

The front door opened and a head peered out, looking around.

We held our breath, frozen in a shadow.

"Shut up, you damned dogs!" came a voice from the door.

Ruff, ruff.

"Shut *up*, goddammit!"

Ruff.

The door closed, and the porch light went out, releasing us from our frozen state.

"C'mon," Catherine whispered.

We put our boots back on and headed back down the road. Mosquitoes were relentless as we passed through the swamp just past Tripp Road. We swatted and hopped around trying to escape them. They let up as we got to higher ground.

Ronnie Clark's house was dark, but a tall pole lamp lit up the driveway and two sides of the small tack barn. Moths and June bugs were busy bumping around the light. We instinctively positioned ourselves in the shadows on the opposite side of the barn, under the tree Holly had been tied to before.

Here's the rub: the only door on the barn was on the side that was lit up like a Polish church. That door was in plain view of every window on that house. This was where our plan ran out. But if this had been easy, you wouldn't be reading this because there would be no story to tell.

"Here, hold this." Catherine handed me the sack. She crawled to the door and pulled gently on the bottom corner. She pulled again, harder this time. Nothing. "It's locked," she said after crawling back to the safe side.

"You said he didn't have locks on his barns," I said.

"He didn't. I guess 'til his stuff started comin' up missing."

In the country, folks didn't generally lock buildings. Barn doors didn't have locks, and even though the house did, nobody even knew where the keys were. Heck, Mom left the car keys in the ignition unless we were in town.

"Dang it. Now what?" I said.

Catherine slumped down against the side of the barn. "We're gonna have to just fess up. If we tell 'em we just wanted to borrow the stuff, maybe he'll understand."

"He doesn't seem like the kind of guy who understands," I said.

"He's only gonna yell at me. What else can he do?"

"He can tell Daddy, that's what."

"He'll yell at me, too, I suppose."

"I'll fess up. I'll say I did it. That I stole the stuff, and that you tried to stop me, but I did it anyway."

"I'm still in trouble. For letting you do it."

"You shouldn't catch it for somethin' I did. That's not fair."

"Yeah, but you're just a kid." She stood up and held out her hand to help me up. "C'mon, let's go home."

"Hang on," I said. "Let me try."

"It's a padlock, dummy. You can't open it."

Being the baby of five, you learn a little something about a false sense of security. As long as I can remember, I've tried every lock out of habit. If something was good enough to have a lock on it, I wanted to see what was inside. My sisters' diaries, my brother's footlocker, Daddy's toolboxes, Mom's desk, cabinets at the doctor's, drawers in the principal's office. That's how I knew that sometimes convenience or just laziness would override the need for security. Sometimes people don't spin the dial on a combination lock, or they leave the key in a padlock. Sometimes if they don't push the lock all the way up, it doesn't catch. Even though it looks locked, all you have to do is pull down, and voilà—open sesame.

I took a deep breath and walked to the door.

"Trisha, get back here!" Catherine whispered.

I stood at the door, looked at the lock, looked at her and back at the lock. I held my breath, squeezed my eyes shut, and crossed my fingers tight.

The lock is open. The lock is open. The lock is open.

With the lock in my hand, I closed my eyes and imagined the lock opening in my hand.

The lock is open. The lock is open. The lock is open.

I pulled straight down on the lock, felt it give and pop open.

"It's open!" I whispered.

"What?" Catherine said.

"It's open!"

She carried the bag over to the door. "Careful. Here, let me do it," she said.

"I can do it!" I said, twisting the padlock. As I lifted it, it slipped from my hand and cracked onto the cement doorway.

We gasped in unison and looked at the house. Catherine grabbed my shirt and pulled me back behind the dark corner of the barn. We waited, listening with our eyes. When we thought the coast was clear, we went back to the door, opening it slowly. The hinges croaked a rusty moan.

Ruff! A single bark came from inside the house.

We ducked behind the open door.

I peeked around the door and saw a light go on in the house. "Light's on," I said. "What do we do?"

She made the *shh* sign and took my hand.

I was ready to run.

She pulled me back to the dark corner of the barn.

"Let's run," I whispered.

"We will, hang on. I have to close the door, or he'll know we were here. Just wait until he goes back to bed."

By this time, the swamp mosquitoes had found us and were chewing on us pretty good. We waited and swatted. Finally, the light in the house went out. I checked my watch: three a.m.

"OK, I'm gonna go put it back and shut the door. You wait right here. Don't move. When I come out, you be ready to run."

I nodded, watching as she disappeared through the open door and pulled it closed behind her. I counted her steps inside the barn. One, two, three. I turned to watch her silhouette through the slats.

Ruff! Another single bark from the house. The light came back on.

"Katie! Hurry!" I whispered through the slats. Peeking around the corner of the barn, I could see shadows moving around in the house. "Katie, wait," I whispered. "Don't move."

The door swung open. It was Ronnie Clark. He leaned out, looking around, squinting under the porch light. "What the fuck are you dogs barking at?" he grumbled. He was wearing just his briefs and a dingy white T-shirt. He stepped back in, letting the door slam behind him. "Fucking dogs." There was a thud and a yelp.

"Be ready to run," Catherine whispered back to me through the slats.

"I'm ready."

I counted her steps across the barn floor toward the door. One, two, three. She opened the door and—

Ruff! Ruff! Ruff! A frenzy of barking came from inside the house.

I went to the corner and lay flat on my belly, my face in the weeds, watching the house.

The light switched back on. The door flew open. Ronnie Clark stepped out onto the porch. "Who the fuck is out there?!" This time he had a shotgun in his right hand. As his eyes adjusted to the darkness, they set firmly on the open barn door. "Well, I'll be goddamned…"

Chk-chk. He cocked his rifle.

Catherine was pinned inside the doorjamb, looking straight at me. I motioned for her to stay. Ronnie Clark turned back into the house. When the screen door slammed shut, I motioned for her to move. She ran back behind the barn and crouched beside me.

Before we could budge, Ronnie Clark was back out the door, jeans and boots on, shotgun in hand, headed straight for the barn. The Dobermans trotted on each side.

"Oh shit!" I whispered. "He's comin'!"

"Let's go," she said.

"He has a gun!" I said.

We froze.

"What the fuck? I know I shut this fuckin' door." He stepped inside the barn and flipped on the light.

White beams of light sliced through the open slats, cutting the darkness in front of us. We could hear his boots clomping around the floor as he rifled through stuff on the workbenches. I reached out and grabbed Catherine's hand. Her eyes were closed. She was praying.

"Well, what do we have here?"

We could hear the jingle-jangle of the pelham bit. In the darkness and in a rush, Catherine wasn't able to hide the bridle like we had planned. I squeezed her hand tighter.

On the back of my head, I felt a series of tiny whooshes of warm air. The dogs had picked up our scent, sniffing and huffing through the slats. I could smell their dog breath as they started whimpering and scratching at the wall. Before

I could move, a claw slipped through, grabbing a lock of my hair, pulling it clean out of my braid, and yanking it through the slat.

"What the fuck are you dumbasses on now?" Ronnie Clark said. "Find a rat or somethin'?"

One of them had a hold on my hair, tugging in strong jerks until the whole lock was yanked from the crown of my scalp. A weak yelp escaped my lips. Catherine clamped her hand over my mouth. Years of Mom roughly brushing and pulling my hair and braiding it too tight had toughened my scalp, but not quite that tough.

"That thievin' little cunt was back for more, eh? She couldn't huv got far." He moved back toward the door. *Chk-chk.*

Dread dropped over us like a net. Catherine turned and hugged me hard to her chest. I could feel her breath on my ear. "I want you to get up that tree, OK? Just like Grandma taught you." Her whisper was so slight, I thought the words were coming from inside my own head. "Get up as far as you can, and you stay there until I come back for you, OK?"

"But..." I could feel my throat tighten like a good cry was coming on.

"I mean it. You get up there and stay put until I come back for you."

She hugged me tighter, kissed my cheek, and let me go. My eyes welled with tears as she grabbed the flashlight and turned to the field. She looked back and mouthed, "Don't cry," jerked her chin toward the tree, then stepped into the corn. She had never kissed me before.

Ronnie Clark's boots clomped toward the door, and the barn light flipped off. "C'mon, boys."

I clambered up the tree, getting up the first couple branches easily. As I got higher, the moon and the light from the porch made it easier for me to see into the field.

Ronnie Clark walked down the length of the driveway. When he reached the road, the sound of his steps changed to include the scratch and scuff of the gravel road. There, I could see him clearly: a rifle propped in his right arm and a beer in his left, the Dobermans obediently at his heel. He set his beer down, retrieved a beat-up pack of Pall Malls from his shirt pocket, and scratched a match on the heel of his boot, all without letting go of his rifle. After several failed attempts to light his cigarette, he said, "Fuck it," and put the pack back in his pocket.

The dogs whimpered anxiously, sniffing the air in my direction.

"Whutcha smell, boys? Huh?" He tossed back the rest of his beer and crushed the can under his heel. He let out a belch and turned back toward the house. "Naaah. Probly just another goddamn woodchuck." He waved his hand at the field. "Go on and git it."

The Dobermans bolted from the road, jumped over the ditch, and went straight toward the tree.

"*No!*" I screamed.

Catherine leaped from her position like a jackrabbit, running straight into the cornfield. The Dobermans saw her and changed course, barking.

"What the fuck!" Startled, Ronnie Clark dropped his rifle. "I'll be goddamned! It *was* her! Git 'er boys!" He picked up his rifle and jogged into the field.

Ronnie Clark was slowed by the cornstalks, but the dogs were not. Even with the moonlight, I couldn't see her once she was in the field. I could only see the tassels on top of the cornstalks shake as she ran by them and then shake again as the dogs followed right behind, like dominoes falling in two lines away from me. When she made it to the clearing, I saw a brief flash of her striped shirt and heard the squeak of metal against wood. She'd hit the fence.

Box wire fence on wood posts was the choice du jour for lining fields to keep deer out. Problem is, they are damn near invisible until you're on top of them. Neighbors told horror stories about snowmobilers and horseback riders coming up wrong against a box wire fence.

The dogs were barking frantically with a high-pitched yelping. Surely they were on her now.

"Catherine!" I cried. "Katie Catherine, come back!"

Ronnie Clark had crossed nearly half the distance to the clearing. Hearing the dogs barking victoriously, he picked up his pace in their direction. "Yeah! Git 'er boys!"

Suddenly, the barking stopped. Just like that. Stopped.

For a moment, even the frogs stopped croaking, and the crickets stopped chirping. The only sound was the night breeze pushing against the broad green leaves of the cornstalks.

"Where the hell are you? Goddamn dogs. Can't see shit out here."

I could see the tops of the cornstalks submit as Ronnie Clark closed in on the clearing. He was just feet from where I had seen her shirt. *Where is she? Why isn't she moving? She must be wounded.* I didn't know how bad the dogs had hurt her, but I couldn't let him get to her with that gun.

"Mr. Clark!" I yelled. "Over here!" And I let out a bloodcurdling scream, just for good measure.

"What the good goddamn?"

The cornstalks started moving again, now in my direction, like a rude guest pushing through a crowded party. "By god, there's two of you little bitches…on *my* property! The fuck kinda game is this?"

The screen door screeched open. "What the hell's goin' on out there, Ronald?"

"Shut up, woman, and git back in that house."

"But I thought I heard a scream."

"Woman, I said git in that fuckin' house before I come up there an'—"

He was now close enough for me to see the light hit his bald spot and closing in fast. Five, four, three, two, one. He was right below me.

"Where the fuck are you? You gonna wish yer momma was here to save you now, ain'cha?" He surveyed the ground and kicked at the weeds we had matted down. He picked up the empty grain sack and looked at it under the light. "Thievin' little…Come back for more and even brought ya a shopping sack, eh?"

As he crossed below me again, I could smell his cigarette. I held my breath, closed my eyes, and crossed my fingers.

Don't look up. Don't look up. Don't look up.

"*There* you are!"

I opened my eyes and looked down. He was staring back at me, right up the barrel of his rifle. Crossed fingers didn't work that time.

"Well, look at that, wouldja. I got a tiger by the tail again." He circled around below me, putting the light at his back, keeping the gun on me. "Well, I don't know, Officer. How was I to know it was a little bitty girl up 'nat tree? Huh? All's I know was my barn was busted open, my *shit* was stole, an' then this fuckin' vermin was up my tree."

"Please, Mr. Clark, I can—"

Chk-chk.

"Girl, there won't be enough left of you to bury…"

"*Clark!*" Catherine yelled from the clearing.

"Oh, now I don't fuckin' believe this!" He turned toward her voice, and his gun dropped down to his side.

"Get away from her!" Catherine yelled. "Get away from her *now!*" she yelled again, holding up the flashlight like a beacon.

"Now whatchoo gon' do to stop me, little britches?"

Pause.

"*We are lambs of God!*" her voice boomed. "*No* weapon fashioned against us shall succeed!"

"Crazy ass…" he muttered.

"This is a warning, Clark! You better leave her alone!" Her voice echoed against the barn. "Proverbs says the evil will not go unpunished!"

"Fuckin' crazy ass little bitches…just like yer momma! Yeah, I heard about that." Pointing up at me, he said, "*You* stay right there, you little brat. I'm comin' *back* for you." He tromped back to the edge of the field with his rifle trained on the voice at the fence line.

Blam. He fired. The shot lit up in the dark and shredded the cornstalks in front of him. Guns never sound like they do on TV. It's more like a pop or a crack, like two bricks smacking together.

"How's that for a warning, you crazy little bitch? Gonna warn me, huh?" He cleared the chamber and walked into the field, toward the beam from the flashlight.

"*Turn back!*" she yelled. "How long will you refuse to humble yourself before God?!" With all due respect to Charleton Heston, my sister delivered that line with more moxie than he ever could.

The screen door creaked open again. "Ronald, what in tarnation is going *on* out there?"

"Woman, I said stay in that fuckin' house."

"Well, what are you shooting at in the dark, Ronnie? Come on back in…You're too drunk to be—"

"Goddammit, woman!" He took a few steps toward the house, the rifle now trained on her. "When I tell you git back in that house, I fuckin' *mean* it. I ain't playin' around, an' this ain't shit for you to be involved in, ya hear? Now *don't* you let me see you come out that door one more time, or I swear to god I'll—"

The screen door slammed shut. Then the storm door. Then the porch light went out. And the rest of the lights in the house.

"This is your last warning, Mr. Clark," Katie Catherine yelled. "Repent and turn back from your transgressions!"

He stomped back into the field, stopping to light another Pall Mall. "Now I'm gonna show you what you git fer stealin' my shit right off my goddamn property. You girls are gonna learn a lesson tonight!"

"*Behold!*" Catherine yelled. "The wrath of God will burst upon the head of the wicked!"

At the clearing, I saw the flash of her striped shirt fly over the fence and disappear into the dark.

30

The End of the Road

You know that feeling when you walk into a room full of people and you just sense that they were talking about you right before you got there? Yeah, me too.

When I was six months old, Mom was hanging laundry in the side yard of our house in Detroit. Daddy was working, and all the kids were playing in the yard. I was lying in a buggy, fast asleep. Mom had to go in the house to answer the phone, so she told Karen to keep an eye on me. Fast forward a few hours. Mom had been distracted by other things when she went in the house—cleaning up, starting supper, etc. Daddy got home from work, and Mom called all the kids in for supper. Everyone sat down at the table.

"Where's the baby?" Daddy asked, gesturing to the empty high chair in the corner.

Collective gasp.

Mom asked Karen. Karen said she told Dan to watch me while she went to the bathroom. Dan said he told Mary to watch me. Mary said she and Catherine had taken me for a walk. She let Catherine push the buggy. Everyone looked at Catherine. She was four years old. She didn't talk very much, so she went to the door and pointed. "Baby," she said.

There, at the end of the road, and about twenty feet from US 12, sat my buggy. Daddy ran out the door and down the road and found me just staring at the sky, playing with my socks, none the worse for wear.

All four kids were spanked that night—even four-year-old Catherine—for leaving their baby sister, Trisha, by the road.

31

Dangerous Places

It took Ronnie Clark a good five minutes to make his way through the field, stopping to light another cigarette, fumbling with his rifle, and muttering more cuss words that I had never heard before. From the tree, I could see his white T-shirt as he stepped into the clearing. He struggled to get over the box wire fence with his rifle. "Fuck! Fuckin' fence!" Eventually, he fell over with a thud, and I couldn't see his shirt after that. I stilled myself to listen but could only hear the rustling of wheat in the next field.

The quiet was pierced by a loud horse whinny.

It was her. Katie was OK. Thank god, she was OK.

She whinnied again, and Admiral answered back to her.

She had lured Ronnie Clark a good distance away, so I climbed down the tree and slipped into the dark of the barn. I had to finish what we came for; I had to hide the bridle.

It had been daylight the only time I was in Ronnie Clark's tack barn, so this time I had to navigate the dark space by memory, like in the Audrey Hepburn movie.

Think, Trisha. Think.

I could smell the pile of sawdust in the left corner and the alfalfa bales stacked against the wall to my right. The tack room was on the other side, kitty-corner from the door. Got it.

One step, two, three, four—my foot hit something big and solid, and I fell smack into it, hitting my knee and then

213

the floor. I reached up to feel a cold curved metal blade, caked with soil. A three-blade plow.

Despite the bucolic image, farms are dangerous places. Kids share horror stories about a cousin who was gored by a bull or an uncle whose lungs were crushed in a tractor rollover. Farmers with a limp or missing digits are walking cautionary tales. I had my fair share of kicks, bites, stomps, and stitches. But what doesn't kill you, right?

Mom had an Avon customer who lost a daughter baling hay when her ponytail got caught in the auger. It snapped her neck at eight hundred RPMs, beating her body against the ground for a full half hour before they found her. By the time her dad made it to the kill switch, there was precious little left of her to bury.

Inside the tack room, I remembered the saddle racks on the left, halters on the right, the big green trunk below—a perfect place to hide the bridle. *See? It was there the whole time... You just weren't looking in the right place.* I opened the lid and pushed aside the stack of blankets on top to cram it down toward the bottom. Something in the trunk squeaked. And moved. Before I could react, something ran up my arm, dove off my shoulder, and ran for cover. We both let out a little screech; I'm not sure who scared who more. Apparently, I wasn't the only vermin stealing from Ronnie Clark's barn that summer.

Behind me, the light in the main room came on. He was back.

I heard banging around and mumbling. Footsteps worked their way around and toward the tack room door. I hopped in the trunk, pulled the blankets over me, and lowered the lid just as the door swung open and the light flipped on.

"Fucking asshole thinks he's gonna point a gun at me?" A female voice. Mrs. Clark? "He's gonna wake up dead one morning, that motherfucker." *Bam!* Slamming cabinet doors and flipping over crates.

"Where the hell is…" *Bam. Crack.* Her feet shuffled to the trunk.

Don't look in the trunk. Don't look in the trunk. Don't look in the trunk.

There was a thud on the lid, but it didn't open.

Exhale.

She stopped moving and went silent. Then I heard a sniffle above me. She was lying on top of the trunk.

"God, how am I ever gonna get out of here?" she cried. "I gotta get away from that sumbitch."

My arm was falling asleep beneath me. I tried to adjust it very quietly, timing it with her heaves and sobs so she wouldn't hear me. As I shifted my weight, I felt something move across my neck. At first I thought it was my pigtail, but this had feet. And whiskers. And friends.

"I gotta get out of here," she sobbed. "I can't take no more of his hands on me."

Hold perfectly still. Don't move, don't make a sound.

Her feet slid off the top of the trunk, and she sighed—that last shuddering sigh that comes when you finish a hard cry. "Well, Proverbs says God helps those who help themselves." Her footsteps one, two, three out of the tack room and one, two, three, four out the door.

Slam.

I counted to ten before bursting out of the trunk, rattling from head to toe with the heebie-jeebies. At the door, I checked the house; the doors were closed, lights off. I made sure to lock the padlock before scrambling back up the tree, a few branches higher this time so he wouldn't find me if he came back.

Blam. I saw the flash in the dark. He was pretty far off now.

"Hey, goddammit!" he yelled.

Chk-chk.

A scream. Her scream.

Blam.

Chk-chk.

Catherine yelled something, but I couldn't understand what she said.

Blam. Blam. Two shots.

Ronnie Clark yelled something, but I couldn't understand what he said.

Then they were both yelling at the same time, but I couldn't make out their words.

Blam. One shot.

No yelling. No sound. No crickets. No frogs. Nothing.

Until I come back for you...
What if she doesn't?
It never occurred to me that she wouldn't come back for me.
Never.
Never.
Never.

I don't know how much time passed. I might have fallen asleep. I didn't think to look at my watch. I didn't feel mosquitoes biting anymore. Or that my knee was smarting and my head was bleeding. I sat, numb, my hands over my ears to stop the ringing of gunshots in my head.

FEE-bee, FEE-bee.
Come back for me.
FEE-bee, FEE-bee.
Come back for me.

It was too dark for birds yet. How long had I been out? Could have been a minute. Could have been an hour.

FEE-bee, FEE-bee. FEE-bee, FEE-bee.
Still half asleep, I responded.
CHICK-a-dee, CHICK-a-dee.
I heard rustling in the field and rubbed my eyes to see.
There was movement at the fence line.

FEE-bee, FEE-bee. FEE-bee, FEE-bee.
CHICK-a-dee, CHICK-a-dee.

And there she was.
Walking out of the cornfield, a Doberman trotting along on each side of her.
She was naked from the waist up, covered in dirt and blood.
Her nose was bleeding and her hair was matted down on one side.
She paused at the edge of the barn and motioned the dogs toward the house.
They trotted off obediently.

"You still there, kiddo?"
"Yeah."
"You OK?"
"Yeah."
"C'mon, let's go home."

An Eye for an Eye

Legend has it that Chief Baw Beese had two daughters—
Waunetta and Winona—who grew up in the hills and dales
of Hillsdale County in the mid-1800s.

When he returned from the River Raisin Massacre in
the War of 1812, he brought a French woman and kept her
as a slave. There is no record of her name, but she bore
him two daughters and died giving birth to Winona. The
girls never knew their mother, but they inherited tragedy
in their blood.

Waunetta fell in love with the son of a French merchant
from Detroit. Before they could be married, he was mauled
and killed on the trail by a mother black bear protecting
her cubs. When Waunetta learned her fiancé was dead, she
rowed a canoe to the middle of Baw Beese Lake, filled her
clothing with rocks, and drowned herself.

Winona was the youngest and the apple of her father's
eye. He openly doted on her and spoiled her with gifts. As she
grew into a young woman, she was described as slender and
fair skinned with bright eyes and long dark wavy hair. She was
wooed by many suitors, but she spurned them all, preferring
her freedom. Eventually, Chief Baw Beese gave his daughter in
marriage to Neguasqua, a member of a neighboring tribe. He
gave his daughter a milk-white pony as a bridal gift. She adored

the pony as much as her father adored her, and she was frequently seen riding it all over the county.

Winona didn't love Neguasqua, but they lived peacefully until he started drinking. Often, he would come home intoxicated and violently abuse her. Adding insult to injury, he began pawning their belongings to pay for his whiskey. When she learned he had lost her prized pony in a card game, she threatened to kill him. He bared his chest and dared her to do it. She took the hunting knife from his belt and plunged it into his heart, and he fell dead at her feet.

Indian law is an eye for an eye. If a member of one tribe murders a member of another, the murderer must die in that same manner at the hand of the victim's next of kin. The two tribes marched to Allen's Prairie, where Winona was bound to a stake. She stood silently as her father made a cross on her forehead and Neguasqua's brother plunged a knife into her heart. After the two tribes built a fire and shared the dance of death, Chief Baw Beese carried his daughter away on horseback and was gone for several days. Legend has it he never told a soul where he buried his daughter. That never stopped a dozen or more families from claiming—to this day—she was buried on their land.

Kids tell each other that if you listen as the sun sets on Baw Beese Lake, you can still hear Waunetta weeping for her lost love. And if you watch the fields when lightning strikes, you can see Winona riding her white pony on the horizon.

33

Losing Daylight

"Betty Lou! Where's my goddamned flashlight?" Daddy barked as he came in the door.

"I don't know, dear. Where did you leave it?" Mom answered.

"Leave it? I left it where it belongs. In my shop, on the wall."

"Did you check there?"

"Would I be asking if it was there?"

"No, dear," Mom answered, never looking up from the stove.

"It's those goddamned kids, I'm telling you," he said. "They get in my garage and take my tools when I'm not here. I told them to keep their grubby little hands off my stuff. They aren't toys."

Catherine and I were setting the table for supper. I looked to her with the question in my eyes—did we return the flashlight? She shook her head no. Jerked her chin west, toward the Clarks'.

Uh-oh.

"Catherine Marguerite? Did you take your father's flashlight?" Mom asked.

"Um...uh...."

"*Did* you?" Mom said, wiping her hands on her apron.

"Um...uh...." she stammered.

"Goddammit! See, I *told* you—" Daddy yelled.

"*I did it!*" I belted out.

"Patricia Anne, you stay out of this," Mom said.

"But I did—I took it."

"What for?" Daddy asked.

"I was building a fort," I lied.

"A fort?" Mom asked.

"Goddammit, I told you to stop building forts," Daddy barked.

"I'm sorry," I said.

"Well, *go* get it," Daddy said.

"Now?"

"Yes, now."

"We're about to have supper," Mom said. "Can't she go get it tomorrow?"

"No, she'll go get it right now. It's gonna rain, and I don't want it to get rusted."

Back on Culbert Road, I could still see our footprints from the night before. The sand hadn't been disturbed since we ran past the McGees' property. Peppermint candy wrappers here and there. The weeds on the bank of the creek were still laid down from where we got in to wash off the blood before going home. We had gotten to the barn as the sun came up. When the other kids got to the barn to do chores, they just assumed we got there first.

The wheat in Ronnie Clark's field was tall and thick, and there were at least two acres to search. How to find a needle in a haystack without him seeing me from the house? When Mary taught me how to do the word search puzzles in the Sunday paper, she said don't try to look at the whole thing all at once. Like mowing a lawn or shearing a sheep, start in one spot and go up and down in neat rows, methodically. So I started at the fence line—farthest from Clark's house—going up and down, back and forth. After a few passes with no luck, I got frustrated and gave up on the method. The sun was going down, and I was losing daylight. I didn't want to get caught, and I really didn't want to let Daddy and Catherine down.

I climbed the best tree on the fence line to get a better view of the field. From that vantage point, I could see a few patches of wheat that had been trampled down. If that's where the tussle happened, that's where she probably dropped the flashlight. It was just dark enough that I couldn't see much at ground level, so I got on my hands and knees, feeling around in the thicker grass. Luck was with me. Finally, the unmistakable ribbed metal shaft handle of Daddy's flashlight came under my hand. When I flipped the switch, it flickered on but then went out. I smacked it with the palm of my hand and thumped it against my thigh, and it came back on. A few steps away, it flickered out again. "Must be the batteries," I muttered and left it off.

Dusk wasn't going to wait, so I kept my eye trained on the horizon and hustled. The rain wasn't waiting either, and even though I didn't mind getting wet, I didn't want Daddy's flashlight to rust. I allowed myself to imagine a grand celebration when I got home. Daddy would be so proud of me when I tell him how clever I was to find it, how I never gave up. He might give me my own bottle of Pepsi. Catherine would tousle my hair and say, "Good job, kiddo." My superior innate ability to find lost things would become part of family legend. *Lost your keys? Ask Trisha. She can find anything.*

Thud.

I tripped and fell. It was one of those falls where you don't catch yourself at all, you just fall clean like a tree. My face came down square on the flashlight. Reflexively, I reached for my eye, smarting and squeezed shut. The flashlight had flipped around and clicked on, shining right in my face. Blinking against the bright light, I was embarrassed and glad no one was here to see me fall.

Once I fetched the flashlight, I looked to see what I had tripped over. It felt soft, almost spongy, like a log that had been in the weather for a long time. Not even hard enough to bruise my shins. The flashlight flickered when I pointed it at the log, but I saw what looked like a bluish color. There's nothing blue in a wheat field. As I stepped closer, the beam of light ran along the log like a finger, up jean-covered legs, a torso, and one outstretched arm.

I fell on my butt and crabwalked backward away from it. That couldn't be. My eyes were playing tricks on me in the dusk light. I stood up and retrieved the flashlight again. It flickered—*smack* and *thump*—back on.

It *was* legs.
It *was* a torso.
It *was* an arm.
And there was his head.
My heart raced, and my breathing stopped. *No, no, no, it can't be him.*
I held my breath, squeezed my eyes shut, crossed my fingers. *It's not him. It's not him. It's not him.*
He was on his stomach, his face straight down. His right arm was stretched out over his head, and his left arm was bent beneath his body. The toes of his boots were buried in the soil, and I saw a flattened path of grass where he had crawled a distance before coming to rest here.
It's not him. It's not him. It's not him.
After making several passes up and down his body with the flashlight, I circled around to his other side and nudged

him with my foot. At his head was a bald spot, a tiny patch of vulnerability. A tattoo on his left bicep was covered mostly in mud, but I could see the foot and recognized it as the *Keep on Truckin'* guy. His right hand was clutching a clod of dirt, and on the back of his hand was the Kewpie doll tattoo.

It's him.

I had never seen a dead body. Sure, I'd seen plenty in Westerns and on the cop shows I watched with Daddy. Kojak and Columbo were always trying to find out who killed this housewife or that gangster. But those were just actors. I'd seen plenty of dead animals. Always tons of roadkill everywhere—raccoons, possums, and squirrels. During deer season, hunters would sometimes hang dead deer in their front yards to bleed out. And we occasionally lost an animal on the farm, a stillborn calf or a piglet crushed by a sow. But never a dead body.

The left side of his head was covered in dried blood and mud, thick enough to cake and crack. His ear was simply gone. I didn't want to see his face, but I needed the confirmation. Crouching down, I tried to push him over, but he was heavy and stuck in the mud. My hands slipped off his wet, slimy skin. I tried again, this time grabbing his belt, and rolled him onto his back.

His right eyelid was glued shut with blood, his nose broken so badly it spread almost flat against his face. His mouth was agape, leaving his tongue to loll out onto his chin. A yoke of blood had dried around his neck and dripped down to his chest.

The flashlight flickered and went out again. *Smack. Thump.* Nothing.

Crickets and frogs began their chirping, just as it started to drizzle.

Out of the corner of my eye, I saw something move and heard a deep gasp, like someone rising to the surface after drowning. A thick gurgle.

Yeah, I screamed. I've always had my mother's nerves. Jumpy. Easily spooked. *But even dead things can move or make sounds*, I told myself. Every farm kid knows about chickens running around after their heads are cut off. Or gases escaping from bloated carcasses. Did you hear that old-timey story about a guy who died sitting up, so rigor mortis set in that way? They stretched him out in his coffin and tied him down. During the wake in the parlor, the family cat jumped on his chest, the rope gave way, and he sat up straight in his coffin, slinging the cat onto someone's lap.

I crouched down by his side, sitting on my heels, and shined the light in his face. I held my hand above his mouth to confirm he wasn't breathing.

He's not alive. He's not alive. He's not alive.

"*Ecch, ecch, ecch...*" He began coughing violently, spurting blood into the air.

Falling back, I dropped the flashlight on his chest.

"Who's there?" he rattled, grabbing the flashlight and holding it like a weapon.

With so much damage to his face, he talked funny, like someone who's just been to the dentist. He couldn't see, so I held perfectly still, even holding my breath.

"Who's that?! I hear you, goddammit!"

"It's just me, your neighbor," I said. "I was looking for my dad's flashlight is all." When I reached for the flashlight, his cold hand clenched my wrist, pulling me down on top of him.

"Let me *go*!" I yelled, trying to yank my arm away.

He swung the flashlight and clocked me right in the mouth. "Gooo...get h-h-help," he gasped, pulling me close. His crossed eye popped open and rolled around, trying to find me in the fading light. His breath smelled like iron and dirt. "P-p-pleeease, sweetie, I'm hurt real bad. Shh...Sheee..." he pleaded, his voice now barely a croak.

"OK, OK," I said. "Let go of me." I pulled my arm, trying to escape his grip.

He squeezed it tighter. "R-r-run...get h-h-help now," he wheezed, releasing my wrist, coughing violently.

I ran. With no real path to follow, I cut straight through the high wheat, keeping my eye on the horizon. "God, please help me! God, please help me!" I repeated, running toward the Clark house. I could still hear him coughing when *wham*—I hit the box wire fence and dropped in a heap on the ground. Hanging from the wire was a small clump of muddy cloth. I saw sleeves, saw that it had been a striped T-shirt, now ripped from neck to navel, soaked in dirt and blood.

I ran back to the clearing with the shirt in my hand, but he was gone.

"Where are you, you bastard!" I yelled. My mouth was still smarting from the hit, my breath still panting from the run, and my mind now racing—how far could he have gotten? I spun 180 degrees with the flashlight, searching like a lighthouse.

I heard rustling behind me. His gurgles and groans led me to where he had crawled further into the wheat.

"What did you do to my sister?!" I yelled.

"Help me—*ecch, ecch*—please," he cried, rolling over onto his back. His left hand flopped down at my feet. In his palm was a clump of dark curly hair.

"*What did you do to my sister?!*" I screamed, over and over, kicking him in the ribs again and again until I exhausted myself and collapsed on the ground next to him. Tears fell hot on my cheeks just as the rain finally started in earnest.

Trembling, he rolled onto his side, facing me and reaching out his arm. "H-h-help...get help. Shh...shh...she *shhhot me!*"

His coughing continued, now more choking and gasping for air. "Please...h-h-help...you...little...bitchhh," he hissed.

Lying on my belly just out of his reach, I pointed the flashlight in his face. His one eye, the crossed eye, set right on me, and the pupil shrank in the light. His breaths were coming in jerks now, fewer and farther between, until they were replaced by a wet crackling sound.

His death was nothing like in the movies. He struggled for several minutes. Could have been hours. I don't know how long, I didn't look at my watch. Finally, his body gave one last shake, his lips curled back in a grimace showing his gold tooth, and the air left his lungs with his soul. I stared straight in his eye as if it would have some answers but got none. He was gone.

My own sobs subsided, and a calm came over me. It wasn't peace or even relief.

It was that I was no longer a child.

34

Enough Trouble

"Who's that sneakin' around in my garage?" Daddy asked.

"It's just me," I answered.

"Me who?"

"Trisha."

Daddy was under a truck, his legs—in greasy overalls—sticking out. I tiptoed in, trying to return the flashlight without him noticing. An air compressor cut off, and Dean Martin was on the eight-track singing "It Had to Be You." He rolled out to get a tool and rolled back under, humming the tune.

"Trisha who? What are you stealin' this time?" he asked.

"Nothing, Daddy, just putting your flashlight back."

"Good. Make sure you put it back right where you found it."

"Yes, sir."

"And you better not have run the batteries dead."

"Yes, sir."

"Don't let me catch you taking my tools again! You hear me?"

"Yes, sir."

I wandered around...

And finally found...

233

Just as I got to the door, "Hey!" he barked.

"Yes, Daddy."

"Come back here."

Uh-oh.

"Get me that wrench right there." He rolled out, but not enough to see me. "Tell your mother I'll be up to the house in about a half hour."

"Yes, sir."

Somebody who…

Make me be true…

Make me be blue…

Catherine had already done my chores by the time I got to the barn. "Did you find the flashlight?" she asked, filling the hay bins.

"Yeah, it was there," I answered.

"No one saw you go back there, right?"

"Um, well…" I mumbled.

"Did you put it back in the garage?"

"Yeah."

"Did you tell Daddy you put it back? He was really mad."

"Yeah."

"What's the matter with you? Why are you acting so—"

I stepped into the light. She saw my face, the black eye, the blood, my lip quivering.

"What the heck? What happened to you?"

I doubled over, crying.

"Are you OK? What happened?" She bent to put her arm around my shoulder, pushing my hair back to see my face.

"I went to get the flashlight—and—and—"

"And what?"

"What happened last night?!" I screamed. "Tell me!"

Her face morphed from concern to anger. "I told you to never ever *ever* ask what happened."

"You tell me right now," I cried. "Please, you have to tell me!"

She lunged at me, grabbed me by my overalls, and knocked me down on my back. She sat on my chest and held my arms down.

"Get *off* me!" I cried.

She put her face in my face, her nose just inches from mine. "You listen, and you listen good," she said. "Don't you *ever* say anything about last night. Do you hear me?" She shook me by my shoulders. "Nothing could ever be more important than this, do you understand?"

"Get *off* me!" I cried. "You're hurting me!"

"I told you before. Don't make me tell you again."

"Please tell me what happened! I don't understand. He—"

Smack.

She smacked my face so hard, my ears were ringing from the blow. She had never smacked me before. "You don't need to understand," she said. "Listen. If you love me, you will keep your mouth shut. It's *over* now, OK? You just keep your mouth *shut*, and I mean it."

Tears and snot were running into my ears.

"Swear it," she said. "Swear on Holly's life that you will never ever say another word. Swear it!"

"I swear," I cried.

"If you ever tell anyone…God will…God will come and take Holly away from you."

"Don't say that! Take it back!"

"It's over now. You got us in enough trouble."

She got up off me. I stayed on the ground, crying. She didn't reach her hand out to help me up like she usually did.

"Now get up and wash your face before you go to the house," she said. "Don't want Mom seeing you like that."

I got up and headed toward the pump house to wash my face. Dan jumped down out of the haymow, landing right in front of me.

"*Aha!* What's wrong, baby? Why are you crying this time?"

"Shut up," I said, still crying.

"Tell me what happened, tell me what happened," he said in a mocking tone.

"Shut up, buttface butthole," I said.

"She finally let you have it," he said, blocking my way. "It's about time. After all the times she took up for you, you little brat."

I swung at him. He moved to miss it, grabbed my wrists, and pulled my face close to his.

"You need to grow up, little girl," he hissed.

I stayed in Holly's stall until everyone else left the barn. She munched on her hay while I cried on her withers. Sarge and McKeever held their posts at her stall gate. Finally, cold and hungry, I went to the house.

"Patricia Anne!" Mom said. "What happened to you? What is on your face?" She took my chin, held it up to the light. "Is that blood? What did you do? What did you get into? And what's that smell?"

"Nothing, Mom," I said.

"Don't you 'Mom' me. Let me see…" She licked her finger and tried to wipe off some blood on my chin. She took me to the bathroom and went at my face with a washcloth. "Open your mouth," she said, pulling out my lip.

"You lost another tooth!" she said, excited. "Well, where is it? You have to put it under your pillow so the tooth fairy will come."

"I don't have it," I said.

"What do you mean you don't have it?"

"I lost it."

"I can see you lost it, but where is it? Where's the tooth? Where were you when it came out? You didn't swallow it, did you?"

My baby teeth never just fell out. I was a chicken about pulling them out, so I would jiggle it with my tongue for days to loosen it until it was literally hanging by a string. Swallowing it was always the fear. My siblings would pester me, asking to pull it for me in the most creative ways, like tying a string around it and tying the other end to a doorknob and slamming the door.

Don't slam the door.

"I must have dropped it," I said.

"Your eye is bruised too," Mom said. "What happened? And what is that smell?"

"I don't know. I'm just a klutz."

"A black eye, a fat lip, and a lost tooth at the same time? Patricia Anne, I know when you're lying. I can see your soul because I am your mother, you know that." She held my shoulders. "You tell me what happened right now. Did someone hit you? Did one of your sisters hit you? Was it Dan?"

"No, Mom."

"Don't you 'Mom' me. They can't hit you. I'll beat the daylight out of…" She dragged me to the living room. "Which one of you did this? Which one of you hit her?"

"Wasn't me!"

"Not me!"

They all wheeled backward, looking at each other, bug-eyed.

She swung me around. "Dan?"

"Catherine did it," Dan said. "I saw her do it. Smacked her good. Little brat had it coming. That's what she gets for sassing everyone."

"Catherine Marguerite!" Mom huffed, turning on her heel, dragging me back to the kitchen.

"Yeah?" Catherine said.

"Don't you 'yeah' me, young lady. Did you hit your baby sister?"

Her eyes darted to me. "I—I—I didn't mean—"

"*Mom*, stop! No one hit me!" I yelled. "Holly...Holly got spooked. Some birds flew up out of the ditch and spooked her. She reared up and hit me in the face." (This would henceforth be my go-to excuse for being late: Holly got spooked and reared up, I fell off, she ran, and I had to catch her.)

"You girls and these horses, I swear," Mom said. "First, your sister comes in all scraped up with a bloody nose from Dusty, and now this."

"It was an accident, Mom, it wasn't her fault," I said, making eye contact with Catherine. "None of this was her fault."

"Well, go get cleaned up," Mom said. "I don't want your father to see you looking like that. And change your clothes—you stink."

It had to be you...

Dear Diary,

I am very scared. Scared Scared SCARED

Why is she being so mean to me?

I will never tell because God would take Holly.

And because I love her. She is my Sister.

I am so so so sorry to get her in trouble.

I know she did it for me. She always protects me.

So I will be very good and never get in trouble again.

And I will protect her secret forever.

God if you are reading this please help me

And please don't take Holly!

Trisha

35

Left Behind

—————•—————

Daddy and I loved gumshoe detective shows. We watched them all: *The Rockford Files, Cannon, McCloud, Baretta.* But our favorites were *Kojak* and *Columbo.* Kojak had swagger and dressed slick. He called people "pussycat" and "cockroach." Columbo was crumpled and slouched. He was a loner, always underestimated.

My two best jokes to make Daddy laugh were:

1. Put a Dum-Dums sucker in my mouth and say, "Who loves ya, baby?"

2. Cross my eyes, pretend I'm writing on a notepad, and say, "Just one more thing…Lemme get this straight."

We would hate on the bad guys, cheer on the good guys, and try to solve the case before the show ended. On *Columbo,* they always show you the crime first so you already know who did it before he ever shows up. The trick is trying to guess which clue the perp would leave behind for him to find.

But most cop shows follow a formula: start with a dead body, determine cause of death, discover evidence, interview witnesses, find the killer and his accomplices, make the collar. Sometimes a piece of evidence is left behind that ties the killer to the dead body. Sometimes an accomplice's face betrays guilt.

Dead men tell no tales, eh? Bullshit. They never shut up. They whisper in your ear; they scream at you in your sleep. And if they're found, they tell everyone what happened.

I had to make sure Ronnie Clark could never tell a single soul.

I had to shut Ronnie Clark up for good.

36

A Place that Doesn't Belong

———————•———————

Everything I know about moving bodies, I learned from Western movies.

John Wayne always threw them across a horse's back, but I wasn't strong enough to do that. Sometimes they were wrapped up like a mummy in the back of a wagon. Then there was the Indian contraption, a travois—long poles dragged on either side of a horse, like a cart without wheels.

Bad guys like Ronnie Clark are usually left to rot in the sun and feed the buzzards, but he needed to be moved to a place where no one would find him. With harvest coming up, he wouldn't be safe in any field. Woods and wetlands would be crawling with hunters in another couple months. Ditches were mowed by the county road commission.

There was only one place in the county where no one would find him. A place that doesn't belong: Christmas Tree Hill.

37

Between Us and Safety

———— • ————

The flies made him easy to find.

The smell made it hard to get close to him.

The house and the road were far enough we wouldn't be seen.

I recognized the sickly sweet smell of rotting flesh, burning my nose and sticking in my throat. We'd had a calf go missing the summer before and didn't find him until he'd been dead for about a week. His leg got stuck in a tangle of fallen branches in the woods across the creek. His black-and-white coat was still soft but couldn't mask the smell of decomposition going on beneath it. When Daddy and Dan pulled him out, his leg came off, holding on by dark-purple tendons.

Ronnie Clark was bloated, his belly now a hideous marbling of yellows and purples pressed hard against his belt. The skin on his arms was translucent, exposing stripes of muscle and vein. His face was dark, and white foam filled his mouth. Maggots hustled in and out of his nostrils.

Holding my breath, I looped the rope in a figure eight around his ankles and tied a good knot. Holly stood calmly while I fixed the rope to the makeshift harness, a collection of clothesline, baling twine, and a saddle girth I pulled together for the occasion. When Mary saw me in the barn earlier making the harness, she asked me what I was up to.

"I'm training Holly to pull a sleigh," I lied.

"But it's summer," she said.

"This is for winter."

"Where are you gonna get a sleigh?"

Pause.

"I'll steal one."

"Ha ha, yeah right."

Maybe I'm biased, but Holly was the best pony. Sturdy, rarely spooked, she did most anything I asked of her. But a harness was new. Not to mention the dead body.

"C'mon, girl," I assured her as we took the first steps. She balked a little when the rope tightened and the harness pressed against her chest, but she trusted me and pulled forward. When I looked back to make sure the rig was holding, his arms were pulled over his head like a grisly marionette puppet.

We were walking, he was dragging. So far, so good.

About a hundred yards into the trek, we ran into a shallow swamp, a narrow strip of knee-deep water and cattails that stretched south from Culbert Road. I looked left and right. There was no way around it. We would have to go through.

As a child in the 1970s, I was leery of swamps because I was terrified of quicksand. Shows like *Gilligan's Island* and *Batman* led us to believe deadly quicksand was lurking around every corner and would swallow you whole.

I hopped on Holly's back—no sense in all three of us getting wet—and gave her a little heel. She craned her neck, huffing at the water and nipping at the tall grasses, but then stepped in. Like I said, really the best pony. The water was already up to her knees just a few feet in. A tiny tinge of instinct warned me to stop before we were in too deep. Dismissing it as fear, I gave her a little more heel.

When I looked back to check on Ronnie Clark, I could only see his toes and his belly button; the rest of him was submerged. *Oh well, ain't no hurting him now, eh?*

Halfway through, Holly slowed to a stop. When I gave her a click or a heel, she would only lean but not take another step. *Oh shit, he's stuck.*

I lowered myself into the swamp water and felt it fill my boots. Holly was content to nibble at the high grass while I checked the cargo. Dipping my hands in the water just above his boots, I felt his wet blue jeans and his belt. It took a long minute to muster the courage to touch his bare skin, I hate to admit. When I did, it was worse than I imagined, and I pulled my hands out several times. "Stop being a baby!" I told myself and finally reached in. Wincing, I felt up and down his arms, shoulders, and torso, searching for where he was snagged. At his waist, I could feel the notch of a submerged branch caught on his belt.

After several attempts, I managed to dislodge the notch by rocking his body back and forth. Not before my hands slipped on his cold, slimy skin and I fell bass-ackwards in the water. Water that wasn't just smelly, stagnant swamp water but now also dead-body soup.

We were only ten feet from the other side, so I walked Holly the rest of the way. When I pulled the lead, she would still only lean but not step forward. The water was now up to her belly. Either the water was rising or Holly was sinking. *Oh shit, it's not him who's stuck, it's her. Quicksand.*

I ran my hand down her front left leg and discovered she was in clay mud up to her knee. With both hands, I dug the mud away from her leg. She lifted it, and I heard a sucking, squelching sound. Then I freed her right leg, but she still couldn't budge because her left leg was stuck again.

"C'mon, girl," I encouraged. She leaned but couldn't step.

I got on her back and kicked her sides hard. "Come *on*, Holly!"
She pinned her ears but couldn't step.

I got off her back and pulled the lead as hard as I could.
"Pull, Holly, pull!"

She stretched her neck but couldn't step.

I pushed her rump, pulled her halter. "Come on, Holly, I
love you. Please try!" I cried.

Think, Trisha, think.

I would have to whip her to get her to move.

At first, I used my hand. I'm sure it stung my hand worse
than it did her rump. She still couldn't step. When I unhooked
the lead rope from her halter, I saw the whites of her eyes. She
was afraid of me and what I was about to do.

I whipped her rump with the lead rope. Once, twice, three
times. She flinched and squealed, like she did when the Clark
boys threw rocks at her. I thought about Little Blackie from
True Grit and Scarlett O'Hara whipping her horse to death. All
my fear, guilt, and shame burst from my chest in heaving sobs.
It was my fault she was here. I deserved the whipping, not her.

If Catherine were here, she would know what to do. She would
know how to get Holly unstuck without having to hurt her. There
was nothing else to do but go back home and get her. Get her to
save me once again. Nothing else to do but face the consequences.

You need to grow up, little girl.

When I got to the bank on the other side, I wiped my muddy
hands on my pants and felt a lump in my pocket. I reached in
and pulled out a peppermint. A sugary truce. Katie Catherine
must have put it there that morning before I got dressed.

Holly's ears perked up at the crinkling of the plastic wrapper. She craned her neck toward me, sniffing.

"You want this?" I asked.

She bobbed her muzzle and leaned forward. I stepped back in the water, crinkling the plastic in my hand. Her eyes got wide, and she gave me a small nicker. I let her smell it, then backed away a few steps, just out of her reach.

Crinkle, crinkle.

"Come on, Holly, you can do it."

She leaned toward me, stretching her neck. I opened the wrapper. She pulled one leg out and stomped it on the water.

"Come on, Holly." I held the candy to her mouth, letting her lips close around it but not letting go. I took one more step back, out of her reach. "Come on, Holly."

She leaned forward, then back, dropping her butt in the water almost as if she were going to sit down. Her rump came back up and—*splash!* Lurching forward, she knocked me back into the water and stepped past me onto dry land. I sat in the water, laughing, and offered the peppermint over my shoulder.

Now that we were out, I could see that spending time in the water didn't do Ronnie Clark any favors. He looked like a swamp creature from an old movie, with green stuff and brown goo stuck on him. The bath improved his smell but only briefly.

While the mud stiffened on our legs, we made good time getting across the field to Tripp Road. We were getting the hang of it. If anyone did see us from the road, they would only have seen a little girl walking through a field with her pony. Truth be told, if my heart hadn't been pounding so hard, I might have forgotten what I was doing and felt like I was just a little girl walking through a field with her pony.

I knew if we could just make it across Tripp Road, the corn in the field on the other side was tall enough to give us cover the rest of the way to Christmas Tree Hill.

Not so fast, tiger.

The tree line on the west side of Tripp Road had a box wire fence. An older line, probably twenty years old, rusty and slouching about a foot off the ground. If it was just Holly and me, we would step right over it as we always did. But Ronnie Clark was not so agile these days. If I couldn't find a way through, we'd have to go all the way around and drag him directly on the road, out in the open.

Leaving Holly to munch, I walked the fence to find a gap.

Please just give me two minutes without a car coming…

Oh great—here comes a car. A green pickup truck. I ducked down, and it passed me, stopping at the intersection. I scurried back to Holly and peeked above the weeds; the truck was still sitting at the intersection. This was unusual because people rarely even stop at a dirt road intersection, let alone wait. I saw brake lights. Then backup lights. The window was down, and an elbow was sticking out. It was Mr. Grosvenor, Bécky Lynn's dad. I crossed my fingers and squeezed my eyes shut.

Please don't stop. Please don't stop. Please don't stop.

"What the hell is going on there?" he yelled out the window.

Please just leave leave leave leave leave.

I stayed down. He couldn't see me, but he could see Holly, munching contentedly.

"What is that goddamned pony doing out there?" he barked, opening his pickup truck door and walking toward us.

I popped my head up. "Oh hey, Mr. Grosvenor!"

"Jesus Christ, what the hell are you doing?" he asked. "You know you're not supposed to be in them fields. How many times do I have to tell you girls?"

"I know…uh…I'm s-s-sorry."

"What are you doing in there? And why are you all wet?" he asked, walking toward me.

"Don't come any closer!" I yelled.

"Why? What are you doing in there?" he said, still approaching.

"I, uh…I'm pooping! I'm pooping."

"Oh Jesus H., you couldn't wait 'til you got home?"

"I couldn't hold it in anymore."

"Damn, girl, whoo! What has your momma been feeding you? Smells like something crawled up in you and died. Pee-yew!"

"I know, I'm sorry."

He got back in his truck. "Finish your business and get the hell out of that field. Don't make me have to call your folks again," he scolded and pulled away, a swirl of dust behind him.

Once he was out of sight, I found a narrow gap in the fence and led Holly through. Back on track, we were halfway there. Just one cornfield between us and safety. Holly nibbled at corn silk spilling out of the ears. The row was a tunnel stretched out in front of me, like that optical illusion where it just keeps getting longer and longer and you're not getting anywhere.

Finally I could see it: Christmas Tree Hill.

The west side of Christmas Tree Hill is much wilder than the east side, where we went sledding. The hill is steep and uneven, and the trees are dense, only feet apart. Dead trees and snags litter the understory. No one had stepped foot in here for years. Maybe since the Indians.

Too dense and wild for sledding, too steep for hunting. Perfect for hiding a body.

If I was gonna shut Ronnie Clark up for good, I would need to drag him deep enough into the trees and cover him well. What I needed was a cave, like in the movies. In *True Grit*, Mattie fell in the cave with the rattlesnake. If it weren't for John Wayne, she'd have never been found. What I found was maybe the next best thing. A massive tree had fallen, pulling its entire root ball out of the ground and leaving a huge hole where the earth had opened up to let it go. An elm tree—the only deciduous tree on the hill—surrounded by fir, pine, and cedar. How had it gotten there? Just like the hill, the elm seemed out of place. Without having other elms around, without establishing a deep enough root system, it never stood a chance.

Holly got Ronnie Clark as close as possible, and I rolled him into the hole like a rug. He landed face down and six feet closer to hell. His back was muddy and scratched deep. The *Keep on Truckin'* guy was almost gone from his shoulder. I gathered what I could find to cover him, and each branch and stick turned his volume down a little bit more.

The only funeral I had been to was my grandfather's when I was three, before I knew about death. I thought he was playing a game. I giggled at him in the coffin and ducked down, playing peekaboo as we had done a hundred times before. At the burial, I ran to his coffin and said, "Gwampa, get out, quit being silly!"

Having now developed a reverence for death, I stood over Ronnie Clark's grave for a long time. Sticks and twigs. It seemed so unceremonial. *Should I say something?* In the movies, the alive people always say something over the dead people when they bury them: "Here lies so-and-so" or "We are gathered here today to honor our beloved." Catherine would have known what to do. She'd have known what to say.

"Dear God, this is Ronnie Clark. I guess you haven't met before," I prayed, looking up to the sky as if I was sure he was watching. "From now on, I won't ask for anything for Christmas or my birthday. All I ask is that you keep Kate out of jail and keep this son of a bitch in this hole. Amen."

38

Mystery and Fodder

A most eccentric man was he,
'tis true beyond a doubt;
they locked him up in Hillsdale jail,
but he managed to get out.

—AUTHOR UNKNOWN

⎯⎯⎯⎯•⎯⎯⎯⎯

Perhaps Hillsdale County's most notorious outlaw was the cross-eyed Silas Doty, "always ready to steal a steed or to sell one; to crack a store or supply one with goods filched elsewhere; to nurse a pal or kill an enemy," according to Michigan poet laureate Will Carleton.

A descendant of the *Mayflower* and the son of God-fearing parents, Silas arrived in southern Michigan in the 1830s, when the region was the wild Midwest: horse thieves and highwaymen, con men and counterfeiters, roving bands of rogues and rascals, murderers and madmen. Silas fit in like a hand in glove.

One of his many grifts was smuggling stolen goods across the Detroit River from Canada, shipping them to Hillsdale by railroad, and selling them on the black market to local merchants. And if the goods were stored in warehouses, he would break in and steal them back. On one occasion, after stealing back stolen horse harnesses from a warehouse, he was caught the next day with the twice-stolen harnesses on stolen horses, pulling a stolen wagon full of stolen goods.

His autobiography tells the tale of being ambushed by a posse after he stole a fine black horse. During the melee, he lost the stolen horse but escaped on foot. He followed the men into town, where he found them drinking in a tavern, whooping about what they would do when they caught him. He took back the stolen black horse and let their horses loose. He joined another posse that was after him and rode with them all the way to Detroit. They were never the wiser.

Doty's life of crime and incarceration was dappled with stabs at redemption. It's rumored that he stole slaves only to free them. Many stories regard him as a bit of a Robin Hood, stealing from his well-off neighbors and giving to the less fortunate. And for a brief period, he tried his hand at an honest life of farming before his nature caught up with him. His hired man found his stash and threatened to blackmail him. Silas beat the man to death with a tree limb and hid the body under a log.

Silas Doty lived to the ripe old age of seventy-six and died peacefully in bed with family around him. "The greatest robber Death had sighted him," wrote Carleton of the outlaw. His obituaries fail to mention his burial site, leaving it a mystery and more fodder for local folklore.

After his death, Silas Doty relics were all the rage. People would travel for miles to see trinkets he had made by hand during his many stints in Hillsdale County Jail and Jackson State Prison (twenty-five years total). A favorite was his bird bottles. Like a ship in a bottle, he built a miniature tree inside a bottle, with tiny carved birds on every branch. Admirers marveled at the patience and craftsmanship necessary to make them.

Pittsford's claim to fame—or infamy—is Doty's Cave, where it is rumored he kept stolen goods. The cave is in Lost Nation, a state game preserve just a couple miles from Pittsford school. Teenagers skip class to look for the mythical site full of hidden treasure, only to give up and spend the day smoking cigarettes in the woods. (Or so I'm told.)

39

Thick and Thin

———————•———————

"What's the matter with you two?" Grandma asked.

"Nothing," Catherine and I said in unison.

Grandma had come to help with canning, and we were all sitting at the picnic table snapping beans. Mom's garden had spread to a half acre at this point, with over fifty tomato plants, onions, green peppers, green beans, peas, pumpkins, watermelons, and several rows of corn. We ate quite a bit of it, and she gave away a lot to her customers, but there was still plenty left to can. She could put up enough to keep us in veggies for the whole winter.

"They're fighting," Karen said. "They haven't talked to each other for days."

"Shut up, Karen," I said. "You don't know anything."

"Don't tell your sister to shut up," Mom said.

"Oh yeah?" Karen said. "Well why are you crying yourself to sleep every night? We can all hear you, ya know."

"Don't say 'yeah,' dear," Mom said.

"What are you fighting about?" Grandma asked.

"Nothing," we said in unison.

"Girls are gonna fight," Mom said. "They'll get over it."

261

"Whatever's come between you, you let it go," Grandma said. "People come and go—friends, boyfriends—but your sisters will always be there for you. Thick and thin. Proverbs says friends love you when things are good, but your sisters will be there when times are tough. That's your blood."

"Like Cain and Abel." Mom laughed.

Inside the house, the phone rang. Mom went in to answer it.

"That goes for all you girls," Grandma continued. "Karen, everything you can do is because Mary believes in you. Everything Mary does is because Catherine believes in her. And what Catherine does is because Trisha believes in her."

"Who's gonna believe in me?" I asked.

"God is holding you, child," Grandma said.

"Girls! Get your boots on," Mom yelled from the door. "This is Vicky Kjellberg on the phone. She says the Clarks' animals are out, all of them. They're all over the county, running on the roads. Someone's gonna get killed."

As we sat in the mudroom pulling on our boots, I searched Catherine's face for how to behave. How to move, to feel. If she was as scared as I was, she didn't show it.

"Mom?" I said from the back seat, once we were on the road. "Did…um…did Mrs. Kjellberg say anything else? Did she say how the animals got out?"

"She says the Clarks must've just up and left," Mom said. "Their house is empty, door's wide open. They're gone."

40

Hardest to Catch

———— • ————

Mom drove us around to look for Ronnie Clark's animals. Catherine was the first to spot Admiral galloping through Shelby's bean field on Beecher Road, pearl white and glossy gray in the sunlight. From the road, we could hear his hooves but couldn't see them, like he was floating and had never touched earth before. His head high, eyes wild, nostrils red. Muscles in his arched neck held his mane like a flag in the wind. No bit in his mouth, no fence around him. He was free.

Be careful, girls—he's dangerous.

Churchill the bull was the smartest of the bunch. He made his way the 1.2 miles from the Clarks' to the Kjellbergs' farm, where he waited calmly next to a pen of curious cows. Big Darryl Kjellberg agreed to hold him until Bud Umholtz could pick him up. Turns out ol' Churchill's bloodline had been with the Umholtz family for generations. They only sold him at auction because they had fallen on hard times, like many farm families did around that time. In exchange for the Kjellberg's hospitality, Bud suggested they leave Churchill in the pen with all available heifers until he could get there. As it might be a few weeks before he could get

265

a trailer big enough to move him, every Kjellberg in a three-county radius would have time to bring their cows by.

It was the mares who were hardest to catch. They couldn't be tempted with buckets of sweet grain. They wouldn't herd but would split off, each going her own way, and seemed unnaturally adept at hiding and camouflaging. In the end, we left their paddock gate open and found them there the next morning. Eleanor Sjogren brought a trailer and took them all back to her ranch, where they belonged.

———————•———————

News of the Clarks' disappearance spread quickly across the county, stirring up a slurry of theories. Most folks just assumed he had failed at the farming life, so they up and skedaddled. But Mom spent the rest of the summer collecting and recycling the more salacious rumors among her Avon customers like a bad version of the telephone game. "Well, I heard they were in money trouble" grew into "They went bankrupt" and eventually "He owed money to a motorcycle gang, so they snatched 'em up."

"I heard they left everything behind."

"The house was empty."

"The house was ransacked, and someone painted satanic symbols on the walls."

"He was running from the law."

"He was an escaped convict."

"I bet he got caught messin' with girls, and somebody's daddy took care of him."

41

By the Feet

————•————

The wives' tale is true: chickens really can run around with their heads cut off. Something about if the butcher cuts too high, the nerves in their spinal cord are still attached, so they can still walk and run.

But they don't get far.

Coming home from the beach at Baw Beese Lake, we could see the feathers blowing around the backyard before we even got in the driveway. White feathers tumbled across the lawn like a hundred ripped-up love notes, pushing against tire swings and tree trunks. As we got closer, we could see the blood. Everywhere, blood. A headless chicken ran across the yard and smacked into a bucket of entrails.

The farmwives were teaching Mom how to slaughter chickens. Grandma Kjellberg would hold a bird down on the picnic table and chop the head off, and the other ladies would take them by the feet. They were using my kiddie pool to strip the feathers and bleed them out. Doris Day was singing "Ain't We Got Fun" on a radio propped up in the window.

"*Mom!* What are you doing?!" Mary said, horrified.

269

"Oh gross, Mom," Karen said and ran into the house.

> *In the mornin'*
>
> > *In the evenin'*
> >
> > > *Ain't we got fun*

The ladies cracked up. "Aw, Betty, you've done it now!"

Mom looked down at herself. Her favorite blue gingham apron with the eyelet trim was generously spattered with blood. Her arms were stained up to the elbow. A small fluffy white feather was stuck in the hinge of her glasses. She looked back at our shocked faces and laughed hysterically. Like bent-at-the-waist, laugh-'til-you-cry laughing.

"Well, kids, where did you think your fried chicken comes from?"

> *In the meantime*
>
> > *In between time*
> >
> > > *Ain't we got fun*

———————•———————

When you grow up on a farm—even a fake farm—you learn to be careful what you get attached to. One day, you might come home and find your mom slaughtering chickens in the backyard. Chickens you raised by hand from tiny peeps. One night, you sit down for supper and Sweetums steaks are on your plate. Sweetums, who you bottle-fed as a calf.

Little Ruby Kjellberg and I were playing with her bunnies on their back porch one day. They were all different colors—some black, brown, and gray, and a white one with red eyes. She took each of them out of the hutch, telling me their names: Opal,

Nibbles, Trixie, Bubba, Mr. Whiskers. We held them on our laps, petting their soft fur and long floppy ears. Eventually, we put them back in their hutch and wandered off to play in the barn, making tunnels from bales of hay and later splashing each other in the water trough. As we were walking back to the house, Ruby took off sprinting when she saw her mom on the porch.

"*Mom!* You promised me!" she screamed. "You *promised* you wouldn't!"

Clumps of bloody fur tumbled down the steps. A skinning knife was stuck upright in the wood railing. Not wanting to see more, I stopped and turned away. Ruby wailed, throwing her little fists at her mom. "I hate you! I hate you!" she cried before stomping up to her room.

"You run on home now," Mrs. Kjellberg said, wiping blood down the front of her gingham shirt. "And tell your folks I said hey."

Dear Diary,

GROSS! Mom was killing chickens in the yard today with the Kjellberg ladies and there was blood all over the place. freaked me out but she thought it was cool.

We went to Baw Beese beach today and I got some tan. Mary got burned again. We put lemon juice in our hair to make blond streaks. I hope mom doesn't notice. She will be mad. The girls both got chiggers again and we had to put nail polish on all the bumps to smother the bugs. *GROSS!* Rusty Schmidt was there and he was flirting with me. Dream on *PUTZ!*

Kelly Kowalski was there too but I didn't see Tammy Latimer??? They are <u>always</u> together but no one has seen Tammy around. Mary heard she got grounded and went up north to spend the summer at her grandmas house. Mom said we might be going to Grandma's cottage up north next month.

T T F N

Karen

42

Just for Girls

"Awww, shee-it! You guys are goin' to jail now!"

The entire bus broke out into murmurs as kids stood up to get a better look at the police car in our driveway.

"Sit *down*, Johnny!" barked Mrs. Pratt, the bus driver. "And quit cussing!" As all five White kids filed past her, she watched each of us step down while her hand was on the door pull. "See you tomorrow, kids," she said. "I'm sure it's all fine."

Bus drivers can see a lot if they bother looking. If a kid is being abused, she's the first one to see the bruises in the morning. She sees if he doesn't have lunch or books or friends to sit with. If a kid is neglected, she's the one who sees him come home to a dark house every afternoon. I can only imagine what Mrs. Pratt thought when she saw the police cruiser in our driveway that day.

My thoughts ran straight to Ronnie Clark.

They found him.

I'm caught.

When we walked in, Sheriff Ramsey was sitting at the dining room table with Mom. He was in full uniform, gray shirt and pants, gun in holster. His big round hat was sitting on the table. Mom had dusted off the Mr. Coffee machine for our guest.

We weren't a coffee-drinking household, but she kept a tin of Sanka and a can of Folgers for company who might prefer a cup of coffee over tea or Pepsi. God knows how old the coffee was or how badly it was prepared, but she made the effort, and Sheriff Ramsey was too gracious to decline her hospitality.

"Hi, Sheriff Ramsey," Dan said, walking through to the kitchen.

"Hi, Sheriff," the rest of us chimed in.

"Hey, kids," he replied.

"How was school?" Mom asked.

"Good," we all responded. Mom never asked us about school, but we played along.

"You kids change into barn clothes before you head back outside for chores. I'm not scrubbing manure out of your good school clothes."

"Yes, ma'am," we all responded. Mom never had to tell us that, but we played along.

Upstairs, we dropped our stuff and changed clothes.

"Kate?" I whispered.

"What?" she replied.

"What's going on?" I asked.

"What?" Catherine answered. "Why are you whispering?"

"What's Sheriff Ramsey here for, do you think?" I asked.

"I dunno," she replied. "Just talking to Mom, I guess. Maybe he's ordering some Avon."

Any other time, I would do everything in my power to eavesdrop on adults' conversation. Especially such an interesting guest who must have the juiciest gossip and the goriest stories. But today I just wanted to slip out the door unnoticed.

"Can I get you more coffee?" Mom asked.

"Aw, no thank you, Mrs. White," he answered quickly, putting his hand over his cup.

"Hey, girls, before you go," Sheriff Ramsey called over his shoulder as we pulled on our boots.

We stopped at the door, trapped.

"Yeah?"

"Don't say 'yeah,' girls," Mom said. "It's 'yes, sir.'"

"Yes, sir?" Catherine said.

"How's that pony working out?" he asked.

"Oh, heh…she's great," I said with a big exhale.

"Yeah?" he asked.

"Yeah," I answered. "Er, uh, yes, sir. I just love her. She's the best pony in the world. We won two blue ribbons at the fair. I'd do anything for her."

"Good, good," he said, nodding. "I'm glad she went to a good home."

"Yes, sir," Catherine said.

Mom reached over to refill his coffee. "She just loves that pony," she said. "You just can't keep those girls out of the barn now."

We took the chance to escape and bolted for the door.

"Girls?" Mom said. "Come here for a minute."

"What about Dan?" Mary said.

"This doesn't concern Dan," Mom said.

"What about me?" I asked.

I was just old enough to get that there are things that are "just for girls," like periods and keeping an aspirin between your knees and a dime in your bra. Those things didn't apply to kids or boys, so this shouldn't concern me either.

"You too, Patricia Anne," Mom said.

She used my full name. She only used my full name if I was in trouble or when she was showing off in the presence of other adults. This could be either. Or both.

Obediently, we lined up at the opposite end of the table, shoulder to shoulder.

"Girls, Sheriff Ramsey has something to ask you," Mom said.

Panic, panic, panic.

"It's about Ronnie Clark," Sheriff Ramsey said. "Did any of you have any…problems with him?"

Panic, panic, panic.

"We only met him a couple times," Karen said, pointing to Mary and herself. "But we didn't really talk to him."

"He stuck his tongue out at Karen," Mary said.

"He did not!" Karen said.

"Yes, he did. He seems kinda creepy," Mary said, wrinkling her nose.

Be careful, girls—he's dangerous.

"Which one of you worked for him?" Sheriff Ramsey asked.

"I did," Catherine answered.

"Did he ever do anything…creepy when you were working there?" He seemed very uncomfortable with how to word his question.

"Like what?" she asked.

He and Mom exchanged glances, like an awkward game of password. "Did he ever say anything…creepy to you?"

"Like what?"

"Did he ever touch you?" Mom butted in.

"Touch me?" Catherine said.

Now I was nervous and uncomfortable in a different way. Scary stuff they don't talk about in front of kids. Just like some of Johnny Carson's jokes, I didn't understand but figured I would someday when I was older. But for now, I just felt icky about it.

"Were you ever alone with him?" Sheriff Ramsey asked.

"Yeah, plenty. Like when I was mucking stalls? Sometimes he was in the barn too."

"Don't say 'yeah,' dear."

"Did he touch you in the barn?" Sheriff Ramsey asked.

Catherine stood silent and still. I reached to hold her hand. "No, he did not touch me in the barn," she said very matter-of-factly, her knee shaking.

"Do you know what to do if anyone touches you?" he asked.

"Kick him in the balls and run," Catherine said.

"Katie Catherine!" Mom fussed.

"Well, that's a good start." Sheriff Ramsey laughed. "And you run straight to your daddy and tell him, OK?"

"OK, that's enough," Mom said. "Run along and do your chores."

The adults continued talking. Catherine and I inched our way to the mudroom, hoping to get outside before they asked any more questions. Catherine stopped at the door, then turned around.

"Mom?" Catherine said.

They kept talking.

"Mom?" she repeated.

"What is it?"

"He touched Trisha."

"What?" Sheriff Ramsey said.

"He touched Trisha. I know he did."

"What? When? How?" Mom said.

"At the fairgrounds, at the auction."

"Patricia Anne, you get back in here right now!" Mom snapped.

She held me by my shoulders. "Did he touch you?"

I looked at Catherine for some explanation.

"It was at the sale barn, that one Saturday," she said. "He did something to her. I know he did."

"He did not!" I said.

"What did he do?" asked Sheriff Ramsey.

"Nothing! I was running, and I ran into him. I spilled my hot chocolate."

"*What* did he do to you, Patricia Anne?" Mom said.

"It was my fault, I ran into him," I said, lip quivering.

"He got her ponytail holder," Catherine said. "He had it."

"Patricia Anne, you tell me right now what happened, and don't you lie," she said, shaking me by my shoulders. Her face was red, her eyes wide and crazy.

"Betty, let me handle this," Sheriff Ramsey said.

By now I was crying. Full-on crying—snot, slobber, the works. Sheriff Ramsey sat me in his chair and knelt down in front of me. He gave me his handkerchief.

"OK, take a deep breath and start from the beginning," he said calmly. "Where were you when he touched you?"

"He didn't *touch* me!" I yelled. "I was running back to the auction because I was gone too long because I was in the tack shop, and I was trying to get back before Mom got mad. He was in the door, and I guess I didn't see him, and I ran into him, and my hot chocolate spilled…and…"

"Slow down, breathe," he said. "And then what happened?"

"I said I'm sorry, and he yelled at me."

"Why didn't you tell me?" Mom asked.

"Because I didn't want to get in trouble."

"Then what?" Sheriff Ramsey asked.

"I ran away."

"How did he get your ponytail holder then?" Catherine asked. "Trisha, tell the truth."

I glared at her, wiping my nose on my sleeve.

"Did he hurt you?" Sheriff Ramsey asked.

"Oh, my baby," Mom said, now also crying.

"I must've dropped it, that's all," I said, still glaring at Catherine. "He didn't hurt me. I was just scared. And I didn't tell you, Mom, because I didn't want to get in trouble."

"In trouble for what?"

"Because you told me to get my hot chocolate and come right back, but I went to the tack shop instead."

"So he didn't touch you?" Sheriff Ramsey asked.

"No. I told you he didn't. He *didn't*," I said, still glaring at Catherine. "I ran into him and fell down, and he yelled at me. That's all."

"Alright, girls," Mom said, wiping her nose. "Go do your chores. And don't slam the door."

Slam.

Outside, Catherine tried to apologize. She held my sleeve and pushed a peppermint into my palm. I yanked my arm away and stomped off. That night, we did our chores separately and in silence. When we got back to the house, Sheriff Ramsey's cruiser was gone. We made sandwiches and ate them in front of the TV. Mom was on the phone, talking to one of her customers.

"Did you hear?...Well, Sheriff says it was more than the one girl...mm-hmm...not just the Latimer girl...Well, they're coming forward now...probably why the family took off like that...We may never know...mm-hmm...No one could believe it...I'm not surprised, what with his filthy mouth...mm-hmm... Yeah, he said that right to my face...mm-hmm...Men like that ought to be locked up...castrate him like a bad bull...Well, I can tell you if Dewey...mm-hmm...if he ever touched one of our girls, Dewey would kill him..."

43
Evolving

———•———

You might say Ronnie Clark was my first love. I was drawn to him. Obsessed. Like picking a scab or the way your tongue can't stop bothering a sore in your mouth, I needed to see him in that hole. I needed to know he was still there, still dead, still mine. Only mine.

I would lie to Mom and sneak away to be with him, as if we were having an affair. Always under the pretense of visiting Becky Lynn, I would ride to Christmas Tree Hill, my head on a swivel to make sure no one saw me. If I was caught, I had excuses at the ready: "I thought I heard a kitten crying over there" or "I'm looking for my hat I dropped when we were sledding last winter." But no one ever caught me.

Sometimes I would imagine that he would be sitting up when I got there, smoking a cigarette, waiting for me. Or worse—the hole would be empty, and he was hiding in the trees over my head, just like I hid from him that night. But he was always there and always dead.

Don't get me wrong, Ronnie Clark was full of surprises.

The first few visits, I would lie on my belly at the edge of the hole and poke him with a stick. The branches and grass had settled into more of a blanket than a roof over him. His outline was there, but everything was under cover except one orange screaming eagle boot sticking out. I needed to feel him, but I didn't want to see him. Not yet. You can forget how something feels but never how it looks. Lots of things feel like a dead body, but nothing else looks like it.

At Halloween time, the older kids would let me help make scarecrows for decoration. We would take some of Daddy's old clothes and fill them with straw, use a pumpkin for the head, and put him in a lawn chair in the front yard. Daddy would come home and yell at us for ruining his "good" clothes. We would laugh and say they were his ratty old clothes that he didn't wear anymore. He would pretend to be mad and say they were his favorites. He didn't wear them anymore because he was saving them for special occasions.

When I poked Ronnie Clark's legs, I was half expecting him to be a scarecrow—that someone had replaced his body with straw. Or that he had filled his own clothes with grass and leaves and was wandering around naked, looking for me.

After a while, Ronnie Clark started getting other visitors. One day, a mama raccoon and her babies were in the hole with him, dining on the maggots and beetles that were dining on Ronnie Clark. Mama hissed at me, and the babies huddled, tumbling over each other and chittering. I thought about petting them, but my fear of rabies kept me at a distance. Well, not rabies so much as rabies shots. Playground mythos said that if you got bit by a wild animal, you had to get a hundred rabies shots in your stomach. Frankly, I didn't even want one.

His other visitors weren't as kind as I was. Some didn't even bother to cover him back up after their visit. Someone made a fast meal of his forearm, leaving the tendons and bones exposed and drying in the sun.

That summer, we had a huge storm, dropping about a foot of rain over a few days. The creeks were at max flow, roads and fields were flooded. When I got to him, Ronnie Clark was floating in his hole like a cracker face down in a bowl of soup. The skin on his back was black, mottled with gray and purple. Ligaments, tendons, and bones were all that was left of his arms. His jeans were sun bleached and threadbare.

Ronnie Clark was evolving.

44

Stealing Grapes

———•———

"Trisha, leave that stuff alone," Dan said.

"Mom! Tell Trisha to quit bugging us," Karen said. "We're trying to do homework."

"Patricia Anne, if you can't behave in there, you can come and sit with me," Mom yelled from the living room. David Brinkley was on the television, speculating about the upcoming presidential debate between President Ford and Jimmy Carter.

The older kids were sitting around the dining room table, working on their current events reports for civics class. They could choose any topic for the assignment as long as it was Michigan related. I couldn't resist rifling through the stacks of Daddy's newspapers and *Time* magazines they had piled on the table.

Dan chose Hank Aaron's 3,298th and final baseball game, played in Milwaukee but against the Detroit Tigers, hence Michigan related. Karen wrote about overcrowding at the Ypsilanti mental asylum, colloquially known as "Ypsi." In Michigan, if you wanted to say someone was acting crazy, you'd say they "escaped from Ypsi," not unlike how New Yorkers refer to Bellevue.

Mary chose the death penalty. That summer, the Supreme Court overruled the previous "cruel and unusual punishment" decision, dividing the country into "an eye for an eye" versus "two wrongs don't make a right." Mary's report focused on Michigan being the first state to abolish the death penalty in 1846. The state's last execution was a tavern keeper who beat his wife to death in a drunken rage. He was hanged on September 24, 1830, outside the jail in Detroit.

"Did you guys know that back in the colonies, you could be put to death for stealing?" Mary said, looking up from her library book.

"Seems harsh," Dan said.

"But only for people who stole a lot of stuff, though, right?" I asked. "Like Silas Doty."

"Not necessarily," Mary said. "Says here that in Virginia, you could be hung for stealing grapes."

"Grapes?"

"And in New York, they would hang you for denying the existence of God."

Pause.

"But not now, right? They don't hang someone for stealing now, right?" I asked.

"No, just for stuff like first-degree murder."

"What does that mean?"

"When you kill somebody on purpose."

Pause.

"But what if they were protecting someone else? If that person could hurt other people, can't someone kill him to stop him?"

"That's still murder."

Pause.

"OK, but what if nobody ever finds out?"

"It's still murder, dummy," Dan said. "They just won't go to prison."

"Still going to H-E-L-L," Mary said.

45

One Little Cowboy and One Little Indian

———•———

Click. "Good mooorning, boys and ghouls." Click.

Principal Dietrich had a pretty good vampire voice on the PA, especially with the canned spooky Halloween sounds in the background—wind blowing, shutters banging, wolves howling. He always dressed like a vampire for Halloween. He was tall and skinny with dark hair and big teeth, so it wasn't much of a stretch. He just drew a little black widow's peak on his forehead and wore a cape over his suit.

Click. "I have a Halloween pop quiz for all of you. Take out a piece of paper and pencil." Click.

We groaned half-heartedly.

"Number one: What is a skeleton's favorite instrument?
"The trombone!
"Number two: What is a witch's favorite subject in school?
"Spelling!
"Number three: What do goblins serve for dessert?
"I scream!" Click.

Poor kids always dressed as ghosts or hoboes. The rich kids always had new costumes from the drugstore: a polyester top and a plastic mask held on with a rubber band. This year's favorites were Superman and Raggedy Ann. Some kids used the same costume every year, and some kids didn't dress up at all.

I was dressed as an Indian girl. Just a hand-me-down that Mom made, a boxy brown felt dress with the hem cut in strips to look like deer hide fringe. With my hair perpetually in braids, it didn't take much to complete the costume. Add a beaded headband, stick a big feather in the back, and smear some war paint on my cheeks.

After morning recess, we had just gotten in our seats when the PA clicked on again.

Click. "*Knock, knock...*" *Click.*

We all yelled out "Who's there?" at the tops of our lungs.

"*Boo!*"

"Boo who?" we yelled.

"*Awww, don't cry, it's Halloweeeen!*" *Click.*

"OK, kids, settle down, settle down," Ms. Abbott barked.

Click. "*One more thing. Can we get Catherine and Trisha White down to the office? Your mom is here.*" *Click.*

The class erupted in the usual jokes about us catching cows. I grabbed my coat and headed down to the principal's office. Catherine was already there when I got to the office. She was dressed as a cowboy: jeans, boots, belt and buckle, plaid shirt, cowboy hat, neckerchief.

"What's going on?" I asked her once we got away from the taunting of our classmates.

Katie shrugged. "I dunno. Probably the cows are out."

"Where's Mom?"

"I dunno."

The secretary finished her call and plunked down the receiver on her pea-green desk model phone. "Girls, your mom's waiting for you in the car," she said and nodded toward the entryway doors. She had the beehive hairdo, the polyester, the blue eyeshadow, the coral pink lipstick. Out of habit, she talked to all kids in her office as if they were in trouble. Her chin down, eyebrows up, head tilted slightly to the right, peering over her glasses.

One little cowboy and one little Indian ambled out the doors and got in the back seat.

"Cows out again?" Catherine asked.

There was no answer from the front seat.

I leaned forward, resting my arms on the back of the bench seat. "Mom? Are the cows out? All of 'em?"

She sniffled and wiped her nose with a Kleenex but didn't answer.

"Where's everybody else?" I asked.

"Mom? Is it the horses?" Catherine asked.

"No," Mom replied and turned around to face us. She had been crying. A lot. Her face was pale, but her nose was red, and her eyes were bloodshot. She looked at us, from face to face, and broke down in a full heaving sob.

As the baby of the family, it was always my job to comfort her when she cried. "It's OK, Mommy," I said instinctively. "It's OK. What's wrong?"

She blew her nose, straightened up, took a deep breath, and put the car in drive. "Just sit back."

We looked at each other and shrugged. In the past, she'd cried like this when she had to tell us about a cat that was hit by a car or a dog that had to be put to sleep. But she wouldn't have taken us out of school for that. Not on Halloween.

When we got to the end of Market Street, she turned left instead of right. We weren't going home to the farm. We were headed toward town.

"Mom, where are we going?" Catherine asked.

"I said just sit back and be quiet," she snapped back.

As we approached the edge of town, Catherine took a deep breath and squeezed my hand. I silently mouthed, "What?" She leaned forward and put her hand on Mom's shoulder. "Mom, I have to tell you someth—"

"Just *sit* there!" Mom snapped. "You can go when we get there."

I pulled her back and mouthed, "What are you doing?"

She looked at me. Her lip was quivering, and her eyes welled with tears. It was happening so fast, I couldn't make sense of what was going on. She whispered, "We have to tell."

"Tell what?" I whispered back.

She looked up and pointed straight ahead. A sign, two blocks ahead on the left. I had been on this road a hundred times and never really noticed it. A big white sign with black lettering:

HILLSDALE COUNTY SHERIFF'S OFFICE

46

Five-and-Dime

---•---

When Dan was four years old, he stole a matchbox car from the five-and-dime. Later, when Mom found the car, she called the police and had them take him to the station in the back of their cruiser. He was left alone in a jail cell for three hours before she picked him up. When they got home, Daddy gave him a spanking.

47

Never the Same

———•———

This was it.

I'd gone over it a hundred times in my head. What we had done was a hell of a lot worse than stealing a tiny matchbox car. There was no getting out of it now.

We were going to jail for what we did.

We held each other's hands in a knot in the back seat. I looked at Catherine. She was praying. I held my breath, closed my eyes, and crossed my fingers tightly.

Make the sign go away, make the sign go away, make the sign go away.

When I opened my eyes, the white sign was gone. I looked out the back window, and there it was. We had passed it! I shook Catherine's hands, but she wouldn't stop praying. She pursed her lips and yanked her hands away but kept her eyes clamped shut. I pinched her knee, and finally she looked up.

"Stop it!" she snarled.

"Lookit!" I said and nodded out the back window. She looked at the sign as it faded away. We both exhaled and collapsed back on the seat.

"You girls sit still back there," Mom said.

It worked again. I had made the white sign go away,

or at least pass us by for now. We would not be going to jail for theft and murder.

Not today.

Mom made a few more turns and pulled into Hillsdale Hospital, parking near the back of the lot. She sat still for a long time after turning the car off, just staring straight ahead and crying. Every time I asked her why she was crying, she would cry harder, so I stopped asking.

Maybe Daddy had had a heart attack and wrecked his truck. Maybe she had cancer. There was always something on the news about cancer. One of the older kids' friends had a mom with cancer. She got really skinny and always wore bandannas on her head. She got better after a while, but she was never the same. And the friend was never the same. Maybe Mom was taking us to the hospital with her so she could tell us she had cancer before she got skinny and bald. Maybe everyone else already knew, and she waited until now to tell us because we were the youngest.

Inside the hospital, she deposited us in the waiting room and went to reception. The lady at the desk was wearing a huge pumpkin brooch and had Halloween bric-a-brac all over her desk. Cardboard skeletons with movable jointed arms and legs were taped up on windows. Crepe paper pumpkins hung from the ceiling. Mom leaned over and whispered something to the lady with the pumpkin brooch. Her expression changed from "How can I help you?" to "Oh, I'm so sorry." She glanced over at us with pity in her eyes and picked up the phone.

"What's going on?" I whispered to Catherine.

"I don't know," she said. "Maybe we have to get our shots."

"We already got all our shots. Remember, we had to get them for school and 4-H?"

"Yeah."

"And why would Mom be crying over shots?"

I just didn't want to believe that I had to get shots. Somehow, it seemed more palatable that my mother had cancer than that I had to get more shots.

"What if Mom has cancer?" I asked.

"What? Mom doesn't have cancer. Stop saying that."

"I didn't say she did. I said what if she did."

"She doesn't have cancer!" she snapped, coming out of her chair.

Everyone looked at us. Pumpkin Brooch looked at us. Mom looked at us. She put her finger to her lips—shh. Catherine sat on her hands, and I flipped through the *Highlights* magazines.

Finally, Pumpkin Brooch called on us. "Mrs. White? The doctor will see you now."

"Come on, girls," Mom said.

One little cowboy and one little Indian ambled into the doctor's office.

4 8

Punishment Fit the Crime

Since moving to the farm, I had been to the hospital four times:

1. After picking up broken glass in the chicken coop,
   I fell backward into a bucket of broken glass and cut
   my left hand. Result: six stitches on my palm and
   pinkie finger.

2. Running on the dirt road, I stepped on a rusty nail that
   went through my little red sneaker and punctured the
   bottom of my left foot. Result: tetanus shot.

3. While playing in a hay loft, I fell through the drop door
   and smacked the top of my head on a beam. Result:
   cracked skull and ten stitches on the crown of my head.

4. Walking barefoot in the barn, I stepped on a
   broken pop bottle submerged in manure and cut
   the bottom of my right foot. Result: eleven stitches
   and another tetanus shot.

Honorable mentions:

1. While sneaking a drink from what I thought was
   Daddy's can of Pepsi, I took a swig from an old

can that had been outside for days. In addition to the putrid liquid, I got a dead bee in my mouth. It stung the inside of my cheek, and my face swelled up like a marshmallow.

2. While riding a boy's bike, I hit a bump and fell onto the bar, injuring my labia. I told Mom I had blood "down there," so she checked and found a small cut. She said this is why girls aren't supposed to ride boys' bikes and told me the punishment fit the crime.

49

Still Intact

·———·

When we got to the room, Mom paused outside the door. She turned to look at us, from face to face, and started crying again. She told me to sit on the bench outside the door. She put her hand on Catherine's shoulder and led her into the doctor's office.

I surveyed my surroundings. No magazines here. No Halloween decorations. Since Mom started dragging me along on her Avon deliveries, I'd gotten really good at entertaining myself in boring places with nothing to do. When I didn't have a book or paper with me, I had to make up games. I counted floor tiles and ceiling tiles. I looked for faces in the patterns the way you look for shapes in clouds.

Some people walked by and smiled at me. "I like your costume," one said. Another guy held up his hand and said, "How," laughing at his own joke. After what felt like an hour, the door clicked open, and Catherine walked out.

Her face was white as a sheet, her cheeks streaked with tears. She didn't look at me.

"What happened?" I asked. "Kate, what happened? Was it more shots?"

She didn't answer or even look at me. Just stood, looking at the floor.

Mom poked her head out the door, wiping her nose with a Kleenex. "Trisha darlin', come on."

"Katie, what's happening?" I said, standing in front of her, but she still wouldn't look at me.

"Patricia Anne, come on. Don't make this any harder than it has to be."

The doctor was writing in a folder when I walked in. Without even looking up, he said, "Have her take her clothes off and get on the table. Knock when you're ready. I'll be back in a minute."

"OK, darlin', let's take off the costume." She pulled the Indian dress off over my head and held up a faded blue gown for me to put on with the opening in the back.

"Mom, what's going on? Do I have to get a shot?"

"No, darlin'. The doctor just needs to look at you. Take off your underwear too."

"My und…But if I take off my undies, my butt will show."

"Take them off."

I slipped them off and immediately wrapped the gown around to cover my butt before climbing up on the table. The doctor came back into the room, still looking down at his file folder. "Are we ready?"

"Yes," Mom said.

I expected the cold stethoscope and the popsicle stick on the tongue. But they didn't show.

"OK, lay back," he said. "All the way back."

Mom took my hand and stood at my side. She looked in my eyes and started crying again. "The doctor needs to look at your…bottom, OK? So just lay back and hold my hand."

He pulled on rubber gloves—*thwap, thwap*—and pulled a silver metal tray on wheels over by my feet. "OK, are we ready?" he asked, putting his cold hands on my feet. My knees instinctively squeezed together.

"Mrs. White, she's going to have to relax."

Mom squeezed my hand. "Just relax, darlin'. It's gonna be OK."

"Let's slide her down," he said.

"Slide down, Trisha darlin'. And relax."

"I'm going to put your feet in these stirrups now, OK?"

Stirrups? These didn't feel like the stirrups I was used to.

"Here we go. Just relax."

Mom held my hand and stroked my forehead. He gently pushed my knees further apart, but I squeezed them back together.

"Mrs. White, I'm going to need her to relax."

"Stop fighting," Mom said. "Don't make it any harder than it has to be."

"Mommy, what's happening?" I pleaded.

"No obvious contusions or bruising on the inner thighs or pelvis," he said. "But there's a tiny scar here on the labia."

"She was riding a boy's bike," Mom explained.

"Ah, that will do it."

I could feel his breath on my thighs. Then I could feel his fingers, cold and slimy.

"OK, we're going to feel a little pressure," he said.

I gasped and looked to my mom with terror.

"It's OK, darlin', it's OK. Just relax."

I tensed up as his fingers pushed and probed. My breath was fast and shallow.

"Tell her to relax, or this is going to be a lot worse than it needs to be."

"Patricia Anne, just relax now. Relax."

I was hyperventilating. My teeth chattered.

"Try to be brave like Katie Catherine was," Mom said.

Oh my god, this is what they were doing to Kate in here. That's why she was crying.

Pride kicked in. I didn't want Catherine to be ashamed of me for being a baby. She was brave, so I would be brave. Staring up at the ceiling, I counted the tiles and looked for faces in the clouds. Breathe in, blow out. I let go of Mom's hand and clenched my hands into fists. Breathe in, blow out. I imagined that I was floating up to the clouds on the ceiling. Just my top half; my bottom half was left on the table. But it wasn't me anymore, so he couldn't hurt me. Breathe in, blow out. Tears had soaked the hair on my temples and were dripping into my ears, so voices sounded like I was underwater.

"OK, almost done here," the doctor said.

"Almost done, darlin'," Mom said. "Just hold real still."

Darlin'? Anger kicked in. Rage. How could she do this? How could she bring me here to let someone do this to me? To Katie Catherine? What did we do to deserve this? To be shamed and hurt and embarrassed like this? Now I really did wish she had cancer. I couldn't think of a death agonizing enough to pay her back for the crime she had inflicted upon me. And on my big sister.

The *thwap* of his rubber gloves coming off snapped me out of it.

"All set here," the doctor said. "You can have her put her clothes back on, and we'll talk."

I was off the table quickly and getting dressed. Mom tried to help me, and I whipped myself away from her. "I can do it my*self*," I snapped.

The doctor came out of his little room with the folder under his arm as I was pulling on my mukluks. "...nothing unusual... both still intact..."

"Oh thank god," Mom said.

Outside the door, I slumped onto the bench next to Katie Catherine. Together, we sat staring at our knees. One little cowboy and one little Indian, betrayed and violated.

The door clicked open, and Mom stepped out into the hall-way, pulling her purse onto her shoulder and wiping her nose with a Kleenex. "Come on, girls, let's go," she said.

Mechanically, we stood up and followed her.

———————•———————

The drive home seemed to take forever. We sat quietly in the back seat, our tearstained faces staring out opposite windows, watching our world go past, one field at a time. Without looking, Catherine reached out and squeezed my hand. When she let go, there was a peppermint in my palm.

In the driveway, Mom said, "Girls, I don't...uh...I thought he must have hurt you. Mr. Clark, ya know." She started crying again. "Just so many girls...I was talking to Mrs. Latimer, and she told me what happened to Tammy. She said she came home with a split lip and a bloody nose, and she said she was really moody, wouldn't talk to anyone. That's how they knew. I thought about how you two have been acting and you coming home all banged up. I thought he hurt you."

Silence.

"Do you know what I'm talking about?" she said.

Silence.

"Well, you'll understand someday when you have your own daughters." She finished crying and collected herself, fixing her face in the rearview mirror.

"Mom?" Catherine said.

"Mm-hmm?"

"Can we go back to school now?"

"Back to…You want to go back to school?"

"Yes, ma'am."

"It's Halloween," I said. "We'll miss the party."

"Well, if that's what you want."

She turned the ignition and drove us back to the school. She dropped us at the front door, where she had picked us up just a couple hours or an eternity before.

"Girls," she said as we got out of the car. "Don't say anything to your father about this, OK?"

"OK," we said in unison.

"Don't tell anyone."

One little cowboy and one little Indian ambled back into the school, however altered. The cowboy made a right, and the Indian made a left, back to our classrooms. And we never told anyone.

Dear Diary,

I HATE HER

I HATE HER I HATE HER

I HATE HER I HATE HER I HATE HER

I HATE HER I HATE HER I HATE HER I HATE HER

I HATE HER I HATE HER I HATE HER

I HATE HER I HATE HER

I HATE HER

Fall 1976

———•———

"Patricia Anne, where are you going?"

"Outside."

Slam.

These days, I was perpetually grounded, but the ground-ings never worked. I still went riding whenever I wanted and came back when I was damned good and ready. A few times, Mom had to send Catherine out to look for me when I wasn't home by dark. I was too young for privileges, and we didn't get an allowance, so she had no chits, nothing to hold over my head. I had something on her, though—

Girls, don't say anything to your father about this.

She couldn't make me stay inside because Daddy would ask why I wasn't doing my chores. She couldn't keep me on the farm because I would just wait for her to go shopping or deliver Avon and then take off on Holly. She couldn't keep me out of 4-H or horse shows because people would notice if only Katie Catherine showed up. She couldn't make me help sort and pack her Avon orders anymore because too much stuff would come up missing. She wouldn't dare scold me in front of other people because I would talk back and embarrass her.

On her birthday, I took her scissors—her good Fiskars scissors—went into the bathroom, and cut off my braids. I left the bathroom with an eight-year-old's sorry attempt at Olga Korbut's ponytails and bangs. School pictures would be swell that year. I put the severed braids in a Kleenex box and gave them to her. "Happy birthday, Mom." I smiled. "I know how much you love my pigtails." She cried and ran out of the room.

While the other kids were cleaning the house, I went to Becky Lynn's. Trotting up the driveway, where I usually turned to go to the barn, I turned toward the yard and gave Holly some heel. It had just rained, so the ground was soft. We galloped around the yard, kicking divots here and there. I pulled her up to a stop and she slid about five feet, leaving deep gouges in the perfectly manicured green grass.

Mr. Grosvenor wasn't going to yell at me for tearing up his lawn today.

Mr. Grosvenor wasn't there.

No one was there.

The whole family had been gone all week, driving to Tennessee for a funeral.

I rode Holly to the back of the house, where no one could see us from the road. I tried the back door, knowing it would be locked. Checking the windows, I found one on the south side of the house that was unlocked. Holly stood still while I used her to climb in the window. Every room was familiar— the light, the smell, the feel of the shag carpet and linoleum floors—but strange and silent without the family there. I sat in Mr. Grosvenor's recliner and put my feet up. I hid his *TV Guide* under a couch cushion. I turned the knob on the antenna. I looked through the fridge and drank out of the juice carton. I took a cherry popsicle from the freezer without asking. I used the bathroom without flushing and snooped through the medicine cabinet.

Upstairs, I started in her sister Kimberly's room. She was a cool girl *and* a bad girl. In a small town, it's easy to be both. Her walls were covered with posters of Bob Seger and Peter Frampton and a fuzzy black-light poster of KISS. A beanbag in the corner was flanked by stacks of *Tiger Beat* magazine. She had every flavor of Bonne Bell Lip Smackers, every color of eye shadow, and a dozen perfumes like Charlie, Musk, and Love's Baby Soft. I sampled a few and rearranged them by height. Her record collection was small but respectable. I flipped past the ABBA and AC/DC and pulled out Elton John. Becky Lynn and I were forbidden to touch Kimmy's record player, but today I turned it up.

> *I think it's gonna be a long, long time…*
> *A long, long time…*

Next, the parents' bedroom, which was strictly off-limits. I had never stepped foot in there, even when there were no adults in the house. We believed Mr. Grosvenor when he threatened that he had booby-trapped the door so he would know if anyone opened it while he was gone. I searched the top shelf of the closet and found Becky Lynn's birthday presents: a small radio, a Breyer horse, and a Connect 4 game. I sat on the bed and felt the satiny bedspread. I took my boots off and got under the covers.

> *Don't let the sun go down on me*
> *Don't let the sun go…*
> *Don't…*

Becky Lynn's bedroom had wallpaper with big purple flowers and a matching bedspread. We must have spent a hundred mornings looking at those flowers and the poster of Leif Garrett above her bed. Who was cuter, him or Shaun Cassidy? I looked through her closet and tried on some of her shirts, none of them hand-me-downs like mine. I found her pink goody bag from period class, filled with tampons and maxi pads. The school called it the "Our Changing Bodies seminar," but everyone called it "period class."

Mom wouldn't let me go to period class. I was the only girl who didn't go, so I had to stay back in the classroom with all the boys. "Why aren't you in period class?" they asked.

"My mom won't let me."

"Why? Don't you know about periods?"

"Of course I know about periods."

"Then why can't you go?"

Mom said I was too young to know, but I already knew. Girls talk. She said it was a mother's job, and it was none of the school's business to discuss such matters with her daughter.

"I'll have that conversation with you when the time is right," she would say.

"When will the time be right?"

"You'll know."

"How will I know?"

Her smile was sinister as she stroked my cheek. "Oh, you'll know, darlin'. You'll know."

I started my period three years later but didn't tell her. And we never had the conversation.

The mirror on Becky Lynn's dresser had a CKLW sticker in the corner and a tie-dye scarf slung over the top. Around the edges, she had stuffed photos, cards, valentines, and magazine clippings into the frame. She had a picture of us at Cedar Point, a picture of us at her mom's softball game, a picture of her family in front of a Christmas tree. And she had a picture of Jenni

Burke, a.k.a. Jenni with an *i*. She was a neighbor Becky Lynn had been friends with since before kindergarten, since before she knew me. Jenni with an *i* had long blonde hair and name-brand blue jeans. She owned her own roller skates and went to a bigger school with newer buses and better sports. They went on field trips to the city. Jenni dotted the *i* with a heart. She always brought the best snacks to Becky Lynn's slumber parties. Jenni with an *i* was always nice to me.

> *Someone saved my life tonight*
> *Someone saved...*
> *My life*

I saw through the window that Holly had munched her way to the front yard. *Shit*. Tidy up, smooth out the bedspread, make sure I didn't drop anything, and dash down the stairs. Before I left, I ran back and took the picture of Jenni with an *i*. I ripped it up and stuffed it in my pocket. On the way home, I scattered the pieces along the road, one by one, like bread-crumbs in a fairy tale.

> *Goodbye yellow brick road*
> *Goodbye...*
> *Goodbye...*

51
A Tooth for a Tooth

———•———

Once the flood water receded, the debris settled at the bottom of the hole, leaving Ronnie Clark exposed and slumped against the side like a discarded doll in the bottom of a toy chest. This was the first time I got a good look at him since I put him there. His jeans were tattered, and one of his boots was gone. His torso and arms were leathery skin draped over bone. He didn't smell as bad anymore.

Though I had felt compelled to bear witness to his gradual demise, until this day I was content to visit Ronnie Clark, poke him with a stick, and confirm he was still in his hole. But the flood left a log wedged just a couple feet over him like a suspended bridge, inviting me to crawl out and get a closer look.

His eyes were long gone, and dirt had settled in the sockets. The eyes he'd used to find my sister in that field were gone. The eyes he'd trained down the barrel of that gun at me. The eyes he'd used to hunt for his victims, that had leered at so many girls, that had watched them squirm and fight. Those eyes were gone, spirited away by bugs and birds.

His mouth was slacked open, his jaw unhinged and resting on his chest. He looked like he was eternally surprised that he was dead, killed by a little girl. *What? I'm dead? How the fuck did that happen?* His teeth were still intact. The teeth that had smiled at so many girls and bit their breasts. The gold one stood up front, and the rest like so many little soldiers holding their posts as they were told. One silver crown had fallen back into his throat, resting now where his spine connected to his skull.

His tongue was gone. The tongue that had made a disgusting gesture at my sisters. The tongue that had said *fuck* to my mother. The tongue that had yelled at Katie Catherine in the field and called her a bitch and a cunt. The tongue that had whistled at so many girls, that had lured them with a ride home and licked their skin while they begged him to stop. The tongue that had enjoyed its very last beer that night was gone. Silenced. Maybe it had fed a family of foxes that he would have shot or poisoned if he wasn't in that hole.

His hands were just bone and some tendon tucked inside translucent gloves of skin. The hands that had beat his wife and kids, that had torn Catherine's striped shirt. The hands that had held down so many girls, covered their mouths, choked the screams in their throats, pulled their braids or their dark curly hair. Those hands had melted into the dirt—dirt that fed worms, worms that fed hawks who carried Ronnie Clark's sins away and shat them on park benches and the windshields of eighteen-wheelers.

The log rolled. My arms and legs wrapped around the log, but my fingers gave out.

Thud.

The last time I was on Ronnie Clark's chest, we were fighting over the flashlight in his wheat field. He called me sweetie and knocked out my tooth. We had both changed so much since then. Now he was small, weak and brittle. But my wounds had since healed, and my grown-up tooth had grown in. He wasn't so scary anymore, but he was still dangerous. A dangerous secret.

The elements were taking him slowly, but he could still destroy me—destroy us—if he was found. A dead bee can still sting.

Be careful, girls—he's dangerous.

I crouched over him, one foot on each side and my face in his. Mother Nature had done her own dental work, but his mercury fillings and silver crowns were plain to see. Like a magpie, I reached into the back of his mouth and grabbed the silver crown and stuffed it in my pocket. It reminded me of Daddy's silver crown, the one you could only see when he threw his head back to laugh. If you saw Daddy's silver crown, you knew you had done good and made him laugh really hard. He loved to laugh, but he didn't do it often enough.

A beam of afternoon sun broke through the pines and lit up his gold tooth. I spit on my finger and wiped the dirt off. It was loose. Without even thinking about it, I dug it out with my pocketknife. The root was nearly twice the length of the tooth itself. It was black and split up the middle. Rotten. Later, in the bathroom mirror, I held it up to my own tooth to see what it would look like in my mouth. A tooth for a tooth, asshole.

———————•———————

When I got home, I went straight to my hiding spot in the hay loft to hide the teeth in my cigar box (where the tooth fairy couldn't find them). Before I dropped them in the box, I took a closer look at the silver crown. I rolled it around in my hand and held it up to the light. Turns out it wasn't a tooth after all.

It was a bullet.

That night, I waited for Catherine to finish her prayers. I could tell when she was finished because she would rub her feet together while she fell asleep, like a bee rubbing pollen off its legs.

"Kate?"

"Yeah?"

"You know how Jesus forgives you for sins as long as you ask him to?"

"Only if you're really sorry for what you did."

Pause.

"Have you ever been really sorry for something you did?"

"Duh," she said.

Pause.

"Wait," she said. "Why are you asking…Trisha…what did you do now?"

"You girls settle down up there," Daddy yelled up the stairs. "Shut up and go to sleep."

"Yes, sir," we said in unison.

After a few minutes passed, Katie Catherine leaned down over the side of her bunk. "Trisha," she whispered. "What did you do?"

"Nothing," I whispered back. "Nothing I'm sorry for."

52

Winter 1976

———•———

It was a stupid game we played as kids. When the phone rang in the White household, we all made a mad dash to answer it. We would leap over furniture, push each other out of the way—tripping was not uncommon. The more dramatic the dash, the better. Since I was the smallest and slowest, I rarely won, but occasionally I was in the right place at the right time, closest in proximity to the phone when it rang.

Like most families in the '70s, we had exactly one phone, and it was centrally located in the dining room. It was a big table model, avocado green. Heavy enough to be used as a weapon if necessary. The cord was long enough to sequester yourself in the stairway if you needed privacy. But that was against the rules, and you could lose phone privileges if you were caught.

In the White household, you must be a certain age before you are allowed to answer the phone. And even after you reach that age, you have to prove that you are capable of answering correctly, using proper phone etiquette. You must be articulate and courteous and be able to answer questions like "Is your mother home, dear?" or "Can you put your dad on the phone?" You answer with "Yes, ma'am" or "No, sir," never "Yeah." And perhaps most importantly, you have to be able to execute the follow-up after you've answered. You can't answer, then get distracted and forget to tell Mom someone was on the phone for her. I did that once or twice and almost lost my phone-answering privileges for good.

When the phone rang that snowy December day, we all leaped for the phone but no one succeeded this time. We were sprawled all over the living room floor, watching *It's a Wonderful Life* on Channel 4, and Mom was winding her beloved cuckoo clock, hung on the wall in the dining room right over the phone table.

"Hello?" she said in her singsongy way. Mom could squeeze four syllables out of the word hello. "Oh, well hello, Miss Missy Melissy!" Mom loved to give nicknames.

At the sound of Missy's Kjellberg's name, we all perked up for our own reasons. Dan because she was pretty, Karen and Mary because she was popular, and Catherine and me because she was a horse girl.

"Uh-huh, yeah, uh-huh," Mom said. "Oh, isn't that nice… Uh-huh, yeah, uh-huh…The kids? Oh, nothing…Uh-huh, uh-huh. Oh, that sounds nice. Hang on, I'll ask.

"Hey, Missy Kjellberg wants to know if you want to go sledding with her and the boys," Mom said.

"*Yeah!*" We all jumped up.

"Don't say 'yeah.' Did you want to talk to one of the girls?" Mom asked. "OK, mm-hmm, mm-hmm. Well tell your folks I said hi," Mom said. "OK then, here's Mary."

"Hi, Missy…Yeah…Yeah…Mm-hmm…OK. Is Gary going? OK. Yeah. Yeah, we have some. OK. See you there. Buh-bye." Mary hung up and said, "Kjellbergs are going sledding at Christmas Tree Hill, and we're invited."

Christmas Tree Hill.

The older kids started getting into snowsuits and boots, pulling on hats and mittens. Mom yelled from the kitchen for everyone to pee before they got bundled up. I was already frozen.

"Hey, kiddo," Karen said. "Why aren't you getting on your snowsuit? Don't you wanna go?"

"I don't know."

"Oh baloney, since when don't you wanna go sledding?"

"I don't know. I don't f eel good."

"Well, get away from me if you're sick."

"Who's sick?" Mom yelled from the kitchen.

"Trisha said she's too sick to go sledding," Mary said.

"I did not!" I said.

"What's wrong?" Mom asked, wiping her hands on her apron. "Are you hot?" She put her hand on my forehead. "Open your mouth and say 'ah.'" She looked at my throat. "Well, maybe you should take some cough syrup just in case."

"Cough syrup? *No!*"

There would be no playing possum in the White household. Any suggestion of illness would be met by a swift counterthreat of cough syrup. Attempts to veil the vile taste in grape syrup failed miserably. To this day, I can still taste it.

"If you're staying home because you're sick, you're going to take medicine, and that's that," Mom said.

The older kids had almost finished suiting up and were heading out.

"See you there. You'll have to catch up with us," Dan said.

"Do you want me to wait for you?" Kate asked.

"Nah, go on. I'll see you there," I replied.

"Not if I see you first!" Dan joked.

"Don't slam the door!"

Slam.

By the time I got into my snowsuit and out the door, the older kids had already gotten the sleds and were well down the road. *Shit. What if they find Ronnie Clark?* I ran to catch up with them, but when I got close, they heard me coming and took off running too, laughing.

When we got there, the Kjellberg kids had already blazed a good trail on the east side of the hill. Two tracks with a fork at the end where you had to dodge a few trees to avoid head injuries. The snow was so deep, they had tied a knotted rope off to the side so you could pull yourself up.

"Hey, you guys," I shouted. "I'm going over here to pee, so don't come over here, OK?"

"Mom told you to go before we left."

"Don't pee on your snowsuit!"

"OK, but don't come over here, OK?" I yelled back.

"Nobody wants to see your ugly butt, dummy."

The east side of the hill got the morning sun, melting a tiny layer on top of the snow, making a crispy layer. Every step made a loud crunchy sound as your feet punctured the icy coating. *Ka-thump, ka-thump.* Looking over my shoulder, I made my way around the hill to Ronnie Clark. He was well covered. Somewhere in that hole, his skull was full, like a grisly snow globe.

Satisfied that my secret was safe, I returned to the group. *Ka-thump, ka-thump, ka-thump.* By this time, they were bored with merely sliding down the hill and wanted to up the danger.

"Trisha, come here, hurry up! We're gonna try to get everyone on the toboggan."

They put me on the front, sitting Indian-style with my legs tucked under the curl. Catherine was behind me with her legs around me, then the girls, then the boys. Heave-ho, and down the hill we go.

The Kjellberg boys were daredevils; there was nothing they wouldn't try. They went down the hill backward, lying down, stacked on top of each other, standing up like they were surfing.

They even brought pilfered cans of WD-40 and PAM to spray the sleds to make them slicker and faster. No matter how hard they crashed, no matter how bloodied or bruised they got, they would pop right back up, laughing and ready to go again. Catherine and I raced up and down the hill with our plastic saucers, trying to get runs in between the big kids. Sometimes they would steal our saucers and try to fold their big bodies onto the tiny circles of plastic. We all roared laughing.

"Mary and Gary, sittin' in a tree, K-I-S-S-I-N-G. First comes love, then comes marriage, then comes Mary pushin' a baby carriage!" Karen and Missy were sitting off away from the group, giggling and laughing.

"What's goin' on?" Dan asked.

"Gary and Mary went off to find a place to neck," Missy said, nodding to a trail of footprints heading over the hill.

I took off following their trail.

"God, Trisha, leave 'em alone, ya little weirdo."

The trail of footprints went up the hill, wound around a few trees, past a couple snow angels, and down the other side. Right toward Ronnie Clark.

"Mary! Maaary!" I yelled out. The footprints disappeared into a tree line and came out on either side of the hole, but Mary and Gary were still nowhere in sight. Now my trails and their trails were going every which way. "Maaary! Where are you?" I yelled.

Behind the felled oak tree, I saw a pair of snow boots poking out, attached to snowsuit legs. I sneaked up and over the tree. There they were. Mary was prone, and Gary was on his side next to her, leaning over in a kiss.

"*There* you are!" I said.

Startled, they sat up quickly, fixing their hats and brushing snow off.

"What are you guys doing?" I asked.

They both blushed.

"What does it look like, we're looking for pine cones," Gary said. "Did you find any?"

"Brat," Mary said. "Come on, let's go back. And don't you dare tell Mom." We started up the hill, and Mary said, "Wait a minute, I forgot my mittens."

She turned back down the hill. Right toward Ronnie Clark.

"Wait! I'll get them for you!" I yelled.

Before I could stop her, she ran down the hill. Just out of sight, she screamed.

We all ran back after her. "What's wrong? What happened?" *Please not the hole. Please not the hole. Please not the hole.*

We got to the bottom. She was in the hole.

"*Help!* Help, I'm stuck!" she yelled.

She had fallen into the big bowl of snow and was clinging to a root sticking out the side. Gary got on his belly and grabbed her arms, pulling her out.

"Kick!" he said. "Push, Mary, push!"

While everyone else was laughing, I was focused on the bottom of the hole.

"Oh my gosh, do you see...What is that?" Catherine asked.

Please stay covered. Please stay covered. Please stay covered.

"It's nothing!" I said, stepping in to block her. "It's just animal bones!"

"No, it's not, silly. Look, right there." She pointed to something on the edge of the hole.

"What is it?" I asked.

She picked up a small bundle of feathers and put it in my hands.

"It's a chickadee," I said. "His neck is broken."

53

And There It Sits

———— • ————

"Patricia Anne! Did you get the mail and newspapers?"

"What?"

"Don't you 'what' me, young lady," Mom snapped back. "Go get the mail and papers."

As usual, after school I dashed from the bus to the house, dumped my books in the mudroom, changed my boots, and was hightailing it to the barn. Mom was in the backyard, hanging sheets on the line.

"You had better go get them before you go to the barn," Mom said.

Back down the driveway and across the road, I got the mail and newspapers. Just as I turned back toward the house, one of the Daugherty brothers flew by in his Bondo buggy and missed me by no more than a few feet. Startled, I dropped everything, and the wind scooped it up and scattered it across the yard. Dashing around, I picked them up one by one: an envelope here, a Publishers Clearing House there. One small envelope tumbled just out of my reach, eventually coming to rest in Mom's fancy rock garden.

Mom and her gardens. Each one was a diorama of what she believed country life to be. She used antique wagon wheels or an old rusty plow as the centerpiece, ensconced in geraniums, chrysanthemums, nasturtiums, and forget-me-nots. She would pose an old metal bucket as if it had spilled purple pansies on the ground. To my mother, the country had become a design scheme. Like motherhood, it was a role for her to play. A smock. Put it on, take it off. Her gardens were based on ideas or ideals she imagined and then manifested. A vision board.

I reached down to fetch that last envelope. It was leaning against a cowboy boot.

One single brown cowboy boot with a screaming orange eagle on the shaft.

Gasping, I lurched backward, dropping all the mail again.

The boot was positioned in front of the wagon wheel, filled with fresh black potting soil. Bright yellow marigolds peeked out of the top, still dewy from being watered.

I looked around to see if anyone else could see it.

"*Mom!*"

Sun was shining through the sheets on the line. Mom was between them, casting silhouettes like the curtains on a community theater stage.

"Bring it here before you take it inside," she said. "I want to see if that check came." She took the stack and rifled through it as I stood there, still panting.

"Uh…Mom?" I said.

"Bills, bills, bills…ugh," she said.

"Mom?"

"There's that catalog! I've been waiting weeks for—"

"Mom!"

"What?"

"Where did you get that boot? The one in the rock garden?"

"Oh, isn't it cute?"

"Where did you get it?"

"I love it. Perfect with that wagon wheel. And the marigolds just set off the orange—"

"Mom, where did you find it?"

"Oh, the dogs came dragging it up the road today," she gestured toward the west.

"The dogs?"

"Mm-hmm. I thought it was just another dead rabbit or something. Then Sarge brought it up on the porch, chewing on it, and I saw it was a boot. Phew—it smelled awful, like something died in it. That's probably why Sarge and McKeever liked it so much. Well, I just thought it would look so cute in that garden, so I cleaned it up, and there it sits."

"W-w-was there anything in it?"

"Oh my gosh, yes. When I reached my hand in there, it nearly scared me to death."

"What was it?"

"A big ol' spider's nest up in the toe of the boot."

"S-s-spiders, huh? That *is* scary."

"Here," she said, handing me the mail. "Take this in the house. And leave the papers next to your father's chair."

"Yes, ma'am."

"And don't slam the door!"

Slam.

Don't Let Me Catch You

HILLSDALE DAILY NEWS

June 13, 1977

REMAINS FOUND

A local man found human remains in a wooded area Wednesday night in Pittsford, sources say. Duane Kjellberg, forty-six, of Osseo, was cutting a felled oak tree just west of Lamb Road when he stumbled—quite literally—upon a human skull, bones, and clothing in a large hole.

"You could have knocked me over with a feather," Kjellberg said. "I've found all kinds of bones before: deer, cow, even coyote," he continued. "But I never seen human bones before."

Police were called to the scene, where they collected the bones and searched for other related evidence.

"It's unclear at this time who the remains are, how they got there, and under what circumstances," said Officer Ralph Edder.

Ronnie Clark was lost, but now he's found.

> I ran.
> I ran as fast as I could to Christmas Tree Hill.

> *I didn't do it.*
> *I only found him.*
> *I don't know who did it.*
> *Did what? I don't even know who it is.*
> *He was dead when I found him.*
> *Catherine didn't do anything.*
> *She was protecting me.*
> *It was all me.*

When I got there, I saw two police cars and a van on Lamb Road. I trounced through the thicket and up Christmas Tree Hill. The sledding run on the east side of the hill was grassy, sunlight pushing through at the top.

"Shh! Get down!" Glenn Kjellberg hissed from behind a tree, motioning for me to get down. The Kjellberg boys must have had the same idea and were trying to find the best vantage point to watch the action without getting caught. But they were way off. I crouched down and made my way over to a crest that looked down onto the hole.

"C'mere, there's a good spot to see from here," I whispered to the boys, close behind me.

"How did you know where to look?" Glenn asked.

"Shh," I replied.

We had missed the best part. From the looks of the hole, they had already removed all the bones. It looked like an empty frosting bowl, licked clean. We watched the police stroll around in the tall grass, kicking through leaves, parting weeds like hair, picking up bits of debris. Occasionally, one guy would find something interesting and yell for everyone to come look at it. Sometimes they would put it in a bag, and sometimes they would throw it back down.

After a while, they got in a group and stood around with their arms folded, talking and nodding for a while before they eventually left the scene one by one. The last one to go was Sheriff Ramsey.

"OK, boys, show's over," he hollered up at us. "You run on home now, and tell your folks I said hey."

"Oh shit!" Glenn said, and they hightailed it out of there.

I dropped to my belly, hoping he hadn't spotted me. *If I can just hold perfectly still until he leaves…*

"Miss White? I know you're there too. Before you go, can you come down here?" he said. "I need to talk to you."

I didn't do it.
I only found him.
I don't know who did it.
Did what? I don't even know who it is.
He was dead when I found him.
Catherine didn't do anything.
She was protecting me.
It was all me.

I slunk down the hill with my eyes on my shoes and my chin on my chest but ready to bolt.

"How're your folks?" he asked.

"Fine," I answered, not looking up.

"How's that pony working out?"

"Fine."

He leaned down, hands on his knees, his face in my face, looking straight in my eyes. "This is serious. I need you to look at me."

I looked at him. He was close enough I could smell his lunch on his breath.

"You know what I'm gonna say, don't you?"

I nodded. Eyes welling up.

You need to grow up, little girl.

"You know I saw you. Out here. In this field."

"I didn't do it." My bottom lip started quivering.

"Don't lie to me. You're not helping yourself by lying."

"Catherine was just protecting me." Tears were falling.

"Catherine? Don't get her mixed up in this. Do you want her in trouble too?"

"No! It was just me. Only me." Now I was bawling with snot.

"You trampled down all those beans. You didn't think anyone was gonna notice?"

"I was scared. I didn't know what else to do."

"Now, come on now, don't cry. You're tougher than that." He chucked me on the shoulder.

"Am I in trouble? What's gonna happen to me?"

"You're not in trouble. Not yet. Tell you what—if you do something for me, I won't tell anyone."

"What?"

He took my hand and led me toward his squad car, parked in the road. "Come with me."

He opened the door to the back seat of his squad car and moved some stuff around. He pulled out a handkerchief and handed it to me.

He took me by my shoulders. "Make me a promise."

"Promise what?"

"Promise me you'll keep that pony out of these fields and stop trampling down these crops. You're runnin' wild out here. I know your dad's already got after you about riding in these fields. You've got so many places to ride, you can't be riding in other people's fields. That's trespassing. And destruction of property. You know that's against the law, right? You don't want to break the law, do you? If I have one more farmer tellin' me about you runnin' in their fields, I'm gonna have to tell your daddy. And I know you don't want that, now do you?"

"No." I blew my nose one more time and gave him back his handkerchief.

"Now you run on home and don't let me catch you out here again. Tell your folks I said hey."

55
The Bogeyman

———— • ————

I had a dream.

Now that Ronnie Clark had been freed from his grave, he was coming for me in my sleep.

I was sitting in the tree outside his barn, watching him walk out of the field. He was skin over bone, his face dirty and bloody, his mouth hanging open. He had the stolen bridle in one hand and his gun in the other.

He walked past me and into his house. The door slammed shut behind him, and the house went dark. Three shots rang out; the light from the gunshots flashed in the windows. He left the house and walked down the driveway, past the barn, to Culbert Road.

I started screaming his name. "Ronnie Clark! Ronnie Clark!" I screamed and screamed, but I couldn't hear my own voice.

The Dobermans were jumping at the base of the tree, barking and gnashing their teeth. I kept screaming. He just kept walking—walking toward my house.

In the dream, I was transported to the tree outside my bedroom window. I could see Katie Catherine. She was lying on her bunk, wearing the striped shirt, torn and bloody. She was sleeping like she always did, flat on her back with her legs pointed straight down and her arms curled around her chest like she was hugging someone. She rubbed her feet together like a bumblebee rubbing pollen off its legs.

Hoofbeats on the driveway. A soft nicker. It was Ronnie Clark, and he had Holly. She was wearing the makeshift harness.

"Get away from her!" I screamed. But I couldn't hear my own voice.

Ronnie Clark started banging on Mom and Daddy's bedroom window. *He's going to tell them what we did.* Then he turned and started climbing the antenna.

Catherine. He was going after Catherine. I had to warn her.

I looked back to the bedroom window. She was still in her sleeping position, but now she was levitating above the bed. I started screaming her name, screaming for her to wake up.

"Catherine! Katie Catherine! Wake up! Catherine, wake up!"

But I couldn't hear my own voice.

When I tried to climb down, the tree kept growing beneath me so each time I got down one branch, another was below me and another and another, and I wasn't getting any closer to the ground.

The light went on in the bedroom. She was still floating above the bed, now praying. Her eyes opened, and her mouth opened in a gasp, as if she was drowning.

"Catherine! Katie Catherine! Wake up! Catherine, wake up!"

Ronnie Clark now stood over her.

"Catherine! Katie Catherine! Wake up! Catherine, wake up!"

Ronnie Clark pulled out a crumpled pack of Pall Malls. He scratched a match across his gold tooth, lit a cigarette, and took a long drag. His eyes rolled up in their sockets, and he looked straight at me. When he exhaled, the smoke filled the room, and I couldn't see Catherine anymore. The smoke poured out of the windows and surrounded the house.

I saw a bright flash of light and—*blam.*

"*No!*" I sat straight up and bumped my head on the bottom of Catherine's bunk. I was drenched in sweat and had bitten my tongue.

"Hey, wake up, kiddo," Catherine said, hanging her head over the bunk. "You're having a bad dream."

"Where is he?" I asked.

"Who?"

"He was just here..."

"Ugh, go back to sleep."

"Kate?"

"What? Just go back to sleep."

"Can I...Can I sleep with you?"

"No! You're too old to be scared of the bogeyman. Go back to sleep."

"But I'm scared."

"Tough. Quit being a baby and go back to sleep."

Jimmy Hoffa

HILLSDALE DAILY NEWS

June 14, 1977

MYSTERY MAN STILL UNIDENTIFIED

The skeletal remains found near a Pittsford bean field have yet to be identified. The medical examiner believes John Doe was a male in his forties, height approximately six feet, based on the femur bone. Some teeth are missing but may have been lost, as animals have scattered and damaged many bones. Cause of death is unknown. No foul play is suspected. No missing person reports in a five-county perimeter match the remains. Anyone with information is asked to contact the Hillsdale County Police.

Ronnie Clark finally got what he wanted—he was the talk of the town. Small-town speculation. Country conjecture. Rumors multiplied like rabbits. Mom talked about it on nearly every phone call and Avon delivery visit. The mystery man dominated every conversation all summer—at church, football games, the grocery store, the feed mill, the supper table. Kids were buzzing about it on the bus, the playground, in the halls at school. Everyone had their theory.

"Carol's son, he works up at the hospital there. Yeah, he does maintenance up there, and you know, that's where the morgue is, so he hears stuff, ya know. Yeah, so he hears a few days back that the bones had been scattered and picked over so much, they don't even know if they'll be able to figure out what killt him."

"Somebody killed that guy and dumped him there. Had to be. Somebody came from the city and dumped him out in the country because they knew he'd never be found out here. Just buzzard bait."

"Hell, maybe he killed himself. Ever think a that? Wouldn't be the first guy to just up and walk out to his field and put the barrel in his mouth. With the economy and the price a grain now, Jesus, who could blame him? Or coulda been cancer. From all the chemicals. Some people don't wanna go through all that, getting sick and losing their hair, havin' their kids see 'em like that. Just end it."

"Not everybody who's dead was killed. Sometimes people just up and die. No reason. Coulda been a heart attack."

"I'd bet anything he got drunker than Cooter Brown and just fell, passed out, snapped his neck. Even if it didn't kill him right away, it'd paralyze him. Oh lord, what if he fell down there, got paralyzed, and was calling for help for days? No one could hear him. Oh jeez."

"Lord willin' and the crick don't rise, they'll find out who he is before the year's out."

"Somebody knows what happened to him. It's happened before, ya know. A couple guys out to hunt camp, start raisin' hell, get careless, and someone gets shot. It happens."

"They're saying the bones were scattered by animals, right? Who's to say he wasn't attacked by a bear or a cougar? Or a wolf, even? DNR says we don't have any out here, but that's bullshit. They just don't want us to know about them, but I swear we hear howling at night."

"Has anyone checked to see if it's Jimmy Hoffa?"

"It's ol' Silas Doty! Nobody ever knew where he was buried. That grave marker just says 'S. Doty,' but that could be his wife, Sophia."

"He was murdered by some nut escaped from Ypsi, you watch. And the sumbitch's still out there."

"Whatever killed him wasn't human. Like a bigfoot who lives out in the woods. It killed him to eat—that's why the government don't tell us about the missing bones."

57

The Scars He Left

———————•———————

HILLSDALE DAILY NEWS

May 1, 1978

INVESTIGATION CLOSED:
Mystery Man to Remain Mystery

Nearly a year after the skeleton of a John Doe was found in a Pittsford field, the investigation will be closed. Authorities say they have exhausted all possible inquiries into the person's identity and the manner of death without being able to reach any conclusions.

"The remains found last summer don't match any missing person reports. And after consulting state medical coroners, they concluded that insufficient evidence exists to support a criminal investigation in connection with those remains," Sheriff Randolph said.

"It's like he just fell out of the sky and into that hole," said a local woman.

———————•———————

353

Was Ronnie Clark finally silenced? Was he in a box on a shelf at the coroner's office? Was he interred at the county graveyard for unidentified persons? Would he ever really be gone?

Ronnie Clark was gone yet everywhere. He had been dismantled and distributed all over Christmas Tree Hill. He fed insects and animals; his hair had made a nest for a whip-poor-will. He was still here. He would always be here, and the scars he left on so many would never heal. Connective tissue would bind me to him as long as the fox that ate his tongue screamed outside my bedroom window.

58

Going to Hell

If I tell you it still haunts me, don't believe me. I'm lying.

You may be surprised to learn that my life just went on as normal after that. No more bad guys, no more bodies, no more black eyes. Not for a while, anyway. Like any other memory, it faded until it didn't seem real anymore. Some days I feel guilty, and some days I'm a hero. Some nights I still lie awake, going over it in my head. And sometimes when I need a boost of confidence—like during a speaking engagement or an argument with my editor—I rub the gold tooth in my pocket, just to remind myself what I'm capable of.

I got away with murder. Well, murder adjacent.

And coveting. And stealing. And bearing false witness against my neighbor.

For a time, I fell short of honoring my mother.

By the age of ten, I had managed to tick off five of the Ten Commandments. I was going to hell for sure, but goddammit, Kate wasn't going to prison.

Make that six commandments.

Epilogue

---•---

"Katie Catherine was my hero. My guiding light. My everything. I spent the first ten years of my life in her shadow. I don't mean that in a bad way. I mean I was never far enough from her to put any light between us. Catherine was the reason I never had to look for monsters under my bed. She saved my life. More than once. In so many ways."

If you find yourself giving the eulogy for your sister, keep it light. Talk about good times.

After high school, Catherine spent a few years training horses for Eleanor Sjogren and competing in show jumping. She won state champion with Admiral. I thought she was happy. She seemed happy. I was happy because I got to visit her and travel with her to some competitions. Then without warning, she was gone. She became a missionary through her church and spent most of the eighties living in developing countries, digging wells and building homes.

I always thought she did it as penance. A penance she didn't know she no longer owed.

We would get postcards from dangerous places. The occasional staticky call from the lobby of a run-down Third-World hotel. After that, she moved on to darker territory, fighting child trafficking in Cambodia and Thailand. Farmers from rural areas send their daughters to the city to make money, where they are then sold to brothels. Catherine's mission put schools and opportunity between the girls and the predators. When they had enough money, they would buy kids—sometimes as young as eighteen months—from the brokers to keep them out of brothels.

In 2003, she caught a rare blood disease. By the time she got back to the states for medical treatment, it was too far gone. God took her quickly.

Walking to my car after the funeral, I felt a small cold hand in mine.

"Catherine saved my life too."

After almost thirty years and behind big dark sunglasses, I didn't even recognize this woman. She motioned me to a bench and asked if I had a moment to talk.

"I have to unburden myself," she said. "Finally, after all these years. After you girls left that night, I took my gun—see, he didn't even know I had a gun. The boys stole it from a neighbor. Just a little snubnose. I told them I wouldn't tell their daddy, that I'd take it back and return it. Only I never returned it. I kept it hidden in the tack room cuz I knew he never went in there. And when he pointed his rifle at me that night, I says to myself, I says, 'That's the last time that sumbitch is gonna threaten my life,' so I went out to the tack barn and got that gun. After a while, a woman has to take matters into her own hands, don't she?"

"Wait…are you…Mrs. Clark?" I asked.

"Call me Angie. Angie Phelps. We were never married.

"Anyways, I sat there all night getting my courage up, but he never come back up to the house. Well, just before sunup, I took the dogs and went out in the wheat field to find him. I knew they could show me where he was and, by god, there he was, laying in the dirt, drunk as a skunk, still holdin' his balls. Your sister must have clocked him good! And his nose was broken, flat over on his face like that." She paused to smile and savor the memory.

"Bastard deserved it. I kicked him in the ribs a couple times to wake him up. I told him I wasn't gonna let him hurt me or the boys or...or...any more of them girls. Not anymore. And do you know, he cried? Sumbitch cried, begging me to help him back to the house. Said if I help him, he'll never lay another finger on me. Well, I fell for that BS before and have the scars to prove it." She turned her head and pulled down her collar, showing a scar stretching from behind her ear down to her throat.

"I told him to go to hell one last time. Then I sent him there. When he went for his gun...well...I shot him. Right in the face. He went down like a brick.

"Ya know, I was raised Baptist. I know murder's a sin—a mortal sin. But I slept better that night than I had since I was a kid, knowing that sumbitch could never touch me again. Or anyone else. Even if I was caught, prison woulda been a vacation compared to what he put me through every day."

"But...how did you know...we...?" I asked.

"The boys. They were watching you out their bedroom window. They saw Katie Catherine run out in the field, and they saw you go in the barn. They told me the next day."

"We were just trying to return the stuff we took. I took."

"I'd have given it all to you girls if I could've. God knows he never used it. Spent all that money on shit he didn't need, and there I was, stuck in the house with nothing.

"But when I went back to bury him...well...he was *gone!*" *Gone* was a whisper. She looked around as if someone might have heard.

"For a while, I figured it was the critters must've got to him, ya know? I kinda liked thinking about the buzzards peckin' his eyes out. Eating his gizzards. I laughed thinking about a coyote chewing his privates off and him just laying there without a dick. Couldn't hurt no one anymore. Oh, pardon my language. I forget where I am.

"But then I figured they wouldn't have eaten his boots and all. And there was nothing there, I mean—*poof*—gone. I went back again and seen a path going into the swamp. That's when I knew—that mean sumbitch survived and crawled off like the snake he is. He'd of holed up somewhere to heal, and then he was gonna come back and get me. An' if he caught me this time, I'd be dead.

"I had to move fast. Me and the boys, we packed up the truck. Before we left, I set all the animals free. They're God's creatures, right? I had to believe that God would take care of 'em better than I could. We drove all night. I dropped the boys off with their mama up in Otsego. That poor woman…"

"They weren't your boys?" I asked.

"No, he took 'em from her. Took 'em out of their beds in the middle of the night just to be cruel. She'd been looking for them ever since. Police wouldn't help because he's their daddy.

"And I've been on the run since. By now, he must've gotten arrested again, probably rotting away in Jackson Prison, right? But as long as he's still out there, I'll never be safe."

"Mrs. Clark, I need to tell you—"

"Uh, please call me Angie. That name, I…I…If I never hear that name again, it'll be too soon."

"Sorry…Angie, yes, I, um…"

"Thank god I had the money. I mean, I've always been able to get jobs and all, but having all that cash has kept me afloat."

"Cash?"

"Yeah, the drug money. See, when Ronald was in Jackson Prison back in '72, his cellmate told him about this big heroin buy in Detroit. Soon as he got out, he went and ripped off the dealer. Almost a hundred grand. He was supposed to share it with his cellie's family, but he shirked them too. That's why we were hiding out in the country. Heck, nothing bad happens there. That's why the boys didn't go to school, why he changed his name and used that stupid Southern accent."

"He did love to flash that cash around," I said.

"You know, I always followed you girls. In the paper. Make sure he never came after you. I saw when you made varsity, saw when Kate took state champion on Admiral. That horse was too good for Ronnie. Hell, I think he was scared of him. But Catherine could get him to do anything."

"She was always good with animals," I said. "Since she was a baby. Daddy always said it was like she could talk to them and they could understand each other's language."

"I was so sorry to hear about your daddy. I bet he was proud when you went in the army. And when Katie Catherine joined the mission. Such a good soul she was, giving her life to save others. Yep, if it weren't for her, I wouldn't be here today.

"Well, I gotta get going. This is the first time I've been back in Michigan since then." She took my hands in hers. "It's been so good to see you and see that you're doing well, but I gotta stay on the run 'til I know he's dead."

I turned her hand over and put the gold tooth on her palm. "He's never coming back for you."

Resources

————•————

The stories of Hillsdale's history were compiled from childhood memory, conversations with family and friends, and various historical references. By far, the best and ultimate guide to Hillsdale's history is *Faded Memories: Examination & Profiles of Hillsdale County, Michigan's Pioneer Period* by Dan Bisher. His unparalleled work illuminates the rich and sometimes dark history of Hillsdale, weaving it into the history of Michigan and the nation.

All lyrics are from songs in the public domain.

Acknowledgments

—————•—————

"You're writing a book? What's it about?"

To a writer, this is the equivalent of someone asking to see pictures of your cat. Over the last ten or more years, I've had the sheer joy of sharing this story with hundreds of people. While most politely feigned interest, a rare few—my butt-kickers— enthusiastically harassed me to finish this book, almost certainly just to shut me up about it. I regret that one very special butt-kicker, Karen Ramsey, left us in 2020 before she had a chance to read my manuscript. Yo, Karen, I did it!

Thank you to my English teachers, Mrs. Knapp, Miss Kolivosky, and Mrs. Perrin. In seventh grade, my writing made Mrs. Knapp cry. In front of the whole class. At the time, I was mortified but deep down I felt the exhilaration of making a reader cry and have been chasing that thrill ever since.

A special thank-you to my beta readers, listed here in alphabetical order: Mary Chapman, Rebecca Hamilton, Mary Hense, Dawn Hoard-Black, Cara Lalley, Rick Lee, Jim Luerssen, Karen Masters, Serene Meshel-Dillman, Jill and Peter Messing, Louisa Moore, Shannon Sclafani, Catherine Spieth, Anna Stania, Corry Westbrook, and Brent and Missy Yarger. And a super-duper special thank-you to the sweet ladies of the Sanilac District Library Book Club, who promised not to hold back, and they delivered. To each reader, I can't tell you how much I appreciate your time and insightful comments. Your positive feedback was received with much gratitude, and your criticism was promptly disregarded.

Thanks to my editor, Chelsea Henderson, who fought really hard to make this a better book while I politely declined most of her suggestions. If you hate this book, blame me, not her. She really tried.

Thank you to the agents who rejected my queries. Publishing my story on my own terms most certainly resulted in a better experience for me and a much better book.

Thank you to everyone at Luminare Press. Your enthusiasm for this book and your support through every step of the process made me feel like a real author.

And finally, thank you to the characters—real and imagined—who came to life in this story. At some point, you just took over, and I was no longer writing but merely documenting your hijinks and capers. I couldn't have done it without you. Now please get out of my head.

Book Club Guide

———•———

This book club guide for Until I Come Back for You *includes discussion questions and ideas for enhancing your book club. The suggested questions are intended to help your reading group find new and interesting topics for discussion. We hope that these ideas will enrich your conversation and increase your enjoyment of the book.*

FOR DISCUSSION

1. How does the small-town, rural setting shape Trisha's story?

2. The story is set in a specific place and time. How does the story touch on larger social issues?

3. The story is told in first person. Did you find Trisha to be a reliable narrator?

4. Does the title fit the story? Where does it play into the story?

5. Trisha and Katie Catherine are very close. How are they alike, and how are they different?

6. What do horses represent to the girls?

7. You meet three generations of women. How does each influence the next?

8. Discuss Trisha's relationship with her mother and how they affect each other.

9. Do you believe it was easier to grow up in the 1970s than today? If so, how?

10. Who are the important men in Trisha's life?

11. Discuss the religious thread in the story.

12. What is the first in the series of events that leads to Ronnie Clark's death?

13. Whose fault is Ronnie Clark's death?

14. How would the story change if it were told from another character's perspective?

15. If this story were made into a movie, who would you cast as the main characters?

16. Discuss the central themes and how they are manifested in the story:

    - Coming of age
    - Faith versus doubt
    - Good versus evil
    - Family
    - Identity
    - Justice

Made in the USA
Columbia, SC
05 April 2025

56116708R00228